The Fractured Halo

The Fractured Halo is a collection of short stories and poems rooted in my experiences as a State Registered Nurse, in South Africa in the 1960s and 70s.

After ten years I returned to England, but Africa constantly beckoned me and I've made the long journey back many times; catching up with old friends, enjoying amazing holidays and more recently as a nurse volunteer in the Townships of the Eastern Cape.

It's easy to describe the wonderful way of life South Africa offered in those days; wall to wall sunshine, houses with swimming pools, barbecues and parties, exotic holidays, good salaries and a low cost of living. But there was a dark side to South Africa ... Apartheid

The Fractured Halo

A Collection of Stories and Poems

from South Africa

JEAN EATON

Copyright and Ordering

Copyright © 2017 by Jean Eaton
All rights reserved. This book or any portion thereof may not be reproduced or used in any manner whatsoever without the written permission of the author except for the use of brief quotations in a book review or scholarly journal.

These short stories are my original creations and names, characters and events are fictional. I have however used real locations for some of the stories to anchor a reference point in time and locality for the clearer understanding of the events portrayed. Similarities to actual persons or events are unintended and I apologise unreservedly if these coincidences cause any offence or embarrassment.

First Printing: 2017
ISBN 978-0-244-35099-4

Anthology compiled, designed and typeset by Bill Cameron
http://www.switchwriters.btck.co.uk.

Cover designed by Bill Cameron from a township photograph by Jean Eaton

Self-published with and printed by LULU Press Inc.

For my daughters
Julia and Katherine

Amelia Thomas

Contents

Acknowledgements --- *2*

Introduction -- *3*

Shacklands --- *9*

The Witchdoctor's Potion ------------------------------------ *11*

Dispossessed -- *44*

The Fractured Halo -- *45*

The Car Jacker -- *62*

Spirit of Africa -- *65*

The Township Line --- *97*

All Roads Lead to Alfonso's --------------------------------- *99*

September Safari -- *116*

What Price a Social Conscience? ----------------------------- *119*

TB The Killer --- *142*

The N2 North to Cape Town ----------------------------------- *143*

Mountain Treachery -- *161*

Ultimate Betrayal --- *163*

The Lost Souls of Umhlanga Rocks ---------------------------- *190*

The Long Road to Humanity ----------------------------------- *192*

The Way to Peace -- *201*

Glossary -- *203*

Acknowledgements

My thanks to everyone who has helped make this book possible. Gillian Baglee for her unstinting support; Patrick Baglee for his wonderful sketches; Karen Lockney for convincing me I could write ; John Mole and Kate Fisher for their encouragement and guidance; Jean Roberts for giving up her time to proof-read, and a special thanks to Bill Cameron for his generosity of spirit in producing this book.

Introduction

The day I sailed into Cape Town harbour, with my husband Richard, remains clear in my mind. How we watched the sun rise over the iconic Table Mountain and gazed in awe as a soft white cloud hovered above its flat top like a table-cloth, before falling in even drapes down the mountainside. And how we marvelled at the sturdy little tug-boats as they steered our ship, the Edinburgh Castle, into port.

I can still visualise the scene at the harbour; a maelstrom of noise and colour. Rows of black faces lined the quayside, waving and cheering. Women balancing baskets of exotic flowers on their heads; vibrant orange and purple strelizias, pink proteas and deep crimson flame-lilies. Plants I had never heard of let alone seen.

At the bottom of the gangplank stomping drummers in leopard-skins beat an ear-splitting welcome and the chitter-chatter of foreign languages added to the vibrancy. It seemed so ... foreign

After almost three weeks at sea I was desperate to post the dozens of cards I had written, so Richard asked a bandy-legged policeman, dressed in a white uniform with a pith helmet, directions to the post office. He grinned at our irrepressible excitement and saluted, "Yes Sir. Welcome to South Africa, Sir," and pointed the way enthusiastically with his truncheon.

But as we moved away from the port area the atmosphere subtly changed. The sun barely pierced the tall commercial buildings. Signs were everywhere; *Slegs Blankes - Whites Only.*

We joined the jostling crowd in the post office. A black official behind a metal grille pointed to me and told me I was in the wrong section, this was for Non-Whites only, I must follow the *Whites Only* sign.

Of course I had read about apartheid, but clearly I had not processed its true meaning. The stark reality was shocking.

That afternoon we headed for the beach, subdued and thoughtful. The sparkling ripples of the Indian Ocean cooled our bare feet as we walked along the water's edge, but embedded in the silver sands the separatist signs flaunted their spiteful message,

Reserved for the Sole use of the White Race Group

I remember how our excitement turned to a pensive silence as we sat in a *Whites Only* bar, drank chilled white wine and watched the grey translucent prawns turn to pink on the barbecue.

I asked the barman where black people went to swim. He told me they had their own areas and pointed vaguely in the direction of the next bay.

I knew Richard had sensed my profound indignation by the way he studiously licked the fiery piri-piri sauce off his fingers, before saying, "Not now Jean, we'll talk later." But we'd both lost our appetite.

Back on-board ship I tried to raise the subject of apartheid with a young South African woman. She told me that it was "just their way of life" and that Blacks were like children, "happy with what they've got". She also warned us not to get involved with politics, that the Bureau of State Security, BOSS, was everywhere and people had been deported for even discussing anti-government views.

I was horrified, but before I could reply Richard had butted in, reminding me that we'd gone to South Africa to work, not get embroiled in politics.

Later, in the privacy of our cabin, we had our first serious disagreement. Richard argued that we couldn't possibly form an opinion after just one day in Cape Town. I felt he was sticking his head in the sand and ignoring the uncomfortable fact that while we were here we would have to live by the country's rules.

I had never imagined that on our first day in South Africa we would experience the unjust, discriminatory sanctions of apartheid.

That night the ship sailed for East London where we disembarked and flew to Johannesburg.

And so began my relationship with this beautiful, complicated South Africa. A country where my children were born; where I witnessed violence, horror and cruelty; where I met the bravest, strongest, most compassionate people of all races, and made life-long friends.

Shacklands

The rich don't go where poor survive,
where sewage runs in rutted tracks
and TB lurks in damp dark shacks
and AIDS a way of life.

No grass, no trees or flowers grow here,
the pigs and cows compete for space,
and mangy curs join in the race
to catch the meatless bones.

The frail old man in borrowed clothes
will greet the day with toothless smile,
and shoeless children all the while
wait patiently for food.

When summer brings the welcome rain,
those rutted tracks will overflow,
and children play in pools below
the leaking tin-roofed shacks.

On Sundays in the tin roofed church
full voices sing in praise of life,
and every day another death
won't shake the people's faith.

The Witchdoctor's Potion

I should have followed my instinct and ignored the advice to hire a 'live-in' maid, but it seemed the right thing to do at the time.

I had known Johannes for six months; he came with the old Dutch-gabled house we rented in the smart suburb of Rosebank, just north of Johannesburg. A six-foot Zulu with hands like spades and feet that overhung his battered sandals, he did odd jobs and kept the acre of garden, including the swimming pool, in immaculate condition. But his main aim in life seemed to be to convince me I needed someone to help with the housework!

I certainly attracted his disapproval when he found me hanging washing on the line. 'Mevrou Annie,' he said, his deep voice incredulous, 'everyone has a girl! How can you possibly go to work, look after the Boss and this house, and not have help?'

Of course, he was right. I couldn't manage the housework! The heavily barred windows needed cleaning, the parquet floors, dulled with dust and paw marks, needed polishing and the ironing was piling up. I think he sensed I was weakening. 'I know a good Xhosa girl who will look after you very well.' he insisted. 'Tomorrow I will fetch her.'

Sure enough, the following morning he was waiting with her by the back door. 'Mevrou Annie, this is Nomano. she has come to work for you.' The girl gingerly stepped forward; she reminded me of a springbok ready for flight, all gangly legs and skinny arms.

'Mevrou,' she said, 'my name is Nomano Mebeke. I am twenty years old and from the Transkei in the Eastern Cape. I am very honest and will work hard for you.' Anxious brown eyes scanned my face, 'My pass is in order, and see,' she pointed to her pink checked overall, 'I have a uniform.'

I gave in. 'Okay Nomano, I'll give you a month's trial. When would you like to start?'

A wide grin, showing perfectly even white teeth, stretched from ear to ear. She glanced at Johannes, eyes sparkling, and giggled, 'Now-now, Mevrou Annie,' she said, holding up her bundle of belongings.'

I sighed. The African concept of time didn't depend on a twenty-four-hour clock; 'now' meant 'maybe later'; 'just now' meant 'later' and 'now-now' meant 'shortly' or 'as soon as I can'. And none was a certainty!

Three months later and I couldn't imagine life without her. Even David, my husband, was impressed; shirts crisply ironed, tennis kit washed ready for Saturdays, and everything he needed for his frequent field trips into the bush laid out on the bed. All he had to do was pack. 'She's even better than my Mother,' he marvelled.

Not much of a recommendation, I thought.

I liked Nomano; she was intelligent, had a good grasp of English, and I discovered she was studying politics and economics in the evenings at the local school. Sometimes we would sit outside on the stoep and discuss the political situation in South Africa and she would tell me about the student movement she belonged to.

'It is all about human rights,' she said, 'about decent housing, good education and health-care, and being treated the same as you.'

Gradually she dropped the formal title, Mevrou, and called me Annie, but I didn't mind.

We spent some hilarious evenings together when David was away; one unforgettable night she tried to teach me how to dance African style.

'You must stick your butt out Annie, like this,' she said, demonstrating a *very* erotic move, 'shake it and then stomp.'

But after laughing hysterically at my pathetic attempts, she decided my 'butt' just wasn't big enough!

However, Estolene, my Afrikaans neighbour and friend, was concerned; as a freelance journalist she could be relied upon to have up-to-date information and sound advice. 'You must not be on such friendly terms Annie,' she warned. 'You don't really know Nomano and I've heard the students are planning to protest against the government's new education policies. She may be involved.' I knew she was right.

I was in the kitchen when Nomano approached me. She pointed to the calendar behind the door and with a red pen circled Saturday, July 16th. 'Annie, on this day I will not be here, I will be at a student rally in Soweto supporting the Black Consciousness Movement. We are demonstrating to force the government to recognise our languages.'

Indignation oozed out of her, 'Why must we be taught in Afrikaans as well as English when we are Xhosa, or Zulu? Africa is *our* country. We *will* fight for our rights.' She handed me a leaflet. On the front I recognised the face of Steve Biko, the black freedom fighter, quoting his famous line: "Black Man You are on Your Own". On the back the inflammatory Soweto declaration: "The School for the Oppressed is a Revolution".

'Okay,' I said, 'but you know there's been a huge police presence at demonstrations recently and many activists arrested. You must be careful.'

But there was something different about Nomano. The way she held her head to one side and stared at me, challenging me to argue with her. She had a new confidence that was almost defiance and met my gaze with a sulky insolence, an expression I hadn't seen before. 'It is just a student rally Annie,' she explained, 'and Johannes will be with me.'

I suspected Johannes was more than just a friend, in fact I was aware he often stayed overnight in Nomano's quarters.

'Annie, this isn't England,' Estolene warned. 'It's against the law for boyfriends, even husbands, to stay in the suburbs or be out after the curfew. You would be in trouble if they are caught and you are seen to be condoning it.' Yet despite her warnings, I acknowledged the injustice of the law and ignored the advice.

Even David, who was so immersed in his job researching water-borne diseases he rarely knew what was going on, was concerned.

'Annie, you know I'm joining a field trip to Mozambique,' he reminded me, 'I'll be away for three or four days. Just remember we're here to work, not solve the country's problems, or challenge the laws.'

Saturday the 16th arrived. Nomano left the house with Johannes to join the demonstration, 'Don't worry Annie,' she said, laughing at my concern, 'there won't be any trouble. I'll be back on Monday.'

It was Sunday evening when Estolene rang. 'Annie, have you heard the news?'

'Not yet Essie. Why? Is there a problem?'

'I heard it on the Afrikaans news this morning; it was a blood bath yesterday in Soweto. More than twenty thousand students attended the rally and the latest figures show many, many students dead, over thirteen hundred injured and many arrested. Have you heard from Nomano?'

'No, but she isn't due back until Monday, I'm sure she'll be okay.'

But by Tuesday I was worried. Nomano still hadn't turned up. I didn't even know where to start looking and Johannes seemed to have disappeared with her. I called Essie. 'She's not back yet, so I'm going to check the hospitals. Don't suppose you want to come with?'

'Okay Annie, I'll be with you just now, I might get a decent story.'

Half an hour later we set off down the drive. As we approached the gates a dishevelled Johannes ran towards us waving his arms, 'Stop, stop,' he shouted, clearly distressed.

I leaned out of the car window, 'What is it Johannes? Have you seen Nomano?'

'Mevrou Annie, on Saturday the police came to the school. They said the rally was over, but armoured cars blocked the roads and the crowds couldn't get away, then the officers started to hit us with batons. Some of the students fought back, some threw stones and sticks. Then the police turned on the tear-gas which made us cough and our eyes sting.

'We tried to run away but they fired bullets into the crowd.' His red-rimmed eyes filled up, 'They were just kids. Some were badly injured and we could hear them screaming in pain, but we couldn't help them, we just had to run. We were almost safe when Nomano was shot in the leg and fell down, so I picked her up and carried on running.'

'It's okay Johannes, take your time.'

Wiping his nose on his blood-stained shirt he carried on, 'A man in a big black car stopped to help us. Blood was pouring from Nomano's leg, so he ripped a sleeve from his shirt and tied it around the wound to stop the bleeding.

Then he picked her up, put her in his car and took us to the Sangoma in Kagiso Township.'

'The Sangoma is the Witchdoctor or Healer,' Essie explained.

I couldn't believe how angry I felt. 'Stupid girl to get so involved,' I stormed. 'Why didn't you stop her Johannes? You knew she could be in danger. And why the Witchdoctor? Why not the hospital?'

'How could I stop her? She was determined to go and so I went too, because she is my girl-friend.' He shrugged, 'And anyway the hospital will ask too many questions.'

'Where is she now?'

'She is hiding in a shack, but her leg is very big and hot; she says you must come and bring your medicines.'

I'd only been in the township a few times and that was as an observer with volunteers from the Red Cross, but I knew I had to do something. 'Okay Johannes, climb in the back, you'll have to show me the way.'

'Annie,' Essie interrupted, 'let's stop for a minute and think about this. The place may be crawling with police, we must have a story. Perhaps you could wear your uniform? Nurses are well-liked and respected in the townships so we're unlikely to be stopped.' Of course, she was right!

Back at the house I changed from shorts and T-shirt into my navy-blue Nursing Sister's uniform, grabbed the first-aid box, a couple of towels and a blanket and scribbled a note for David who was due back from his field trip.

David, I've gone to Kagiso to fetch Nomano. Essie and Johannes are with me. You can get me on the radio. Annie xx.

I knew he wouldn't be happy, but what could I do in the circumstances? And anyway, he'd long since stopped trying to curb my impulsive nature.

An hour later Johannes directed us off the main Ontdekkers road into Kagiso. My fingers tightened around the steering wheel and I forced myself to concentrate. No-one spoke as we passed signs of the riots; debris, overturned cars, burned-out shacks. We passed a few police cars, but they didn't stop us and we drove steadily into the heart of the township.

Essie broke the silence, 'Oh God Annie, listen, I think we're in for a storm.' From across the rows of tin roofs I could just hear the first low rumblings of thunder; within minutes the clouds rolled in shrouding the sun and a crack of thunder snapped us out of our anxious reverie. Streaks of lightening divided the sky, shocking the clouds into releasing sheets of rain, and the rutted tracks became muddy streams. The dongas, unable to cope with the deluge, started to overflow and the tyres struggled to grip the slippery surface.

Essie was clearly worried, 'Bloody hell Annie, this is a corker, do you think we should carry on?'

An anxious Johannes leaned forward, 'It is not far now,' he said, pointing to the crossroads. 'There! Go down there.'

I glanced in the rear-view mirror and signalled left. Almost immediately a blue light flashed a warning and a screaming siren ordered me to stop.

I took a deep breath and wound the window down. If everything wasn't in order Johannes could be arrested and fined, even go to prison.

'Good afternoon Officer,' I said, trying to keep my tone calm and polite, 'is there a problem?'

He peered inside the car. 'Sister,' acknowledging my uniform, 'there is trouble in the Township. Waar gaan sie?'

'Just to the Clinic, I'm helping Sister Thembu with the vaccinations.'

He nodded, then turned to Essie, 'And you Mevrou?'

'Goeie dag Officer, good day,' lapsing into her native Afrikaans and smiling at him. 'I'll be working with Sister Annie, she kindly offered to show me the clinic.'

I nearly choked as the lies tripped off her tongue. He wouldn't be too happy if he knew she was a journalist!

The officer snapped open his baton and walked round to the off-side rear door. 'You, Kaffir,' he ordered, 'out. Show me your pass.' Johannes slid out of the car and pulled his collar up against the rain. He opened his mouth as if to speak, but no words came out.

The officer pushed him face down over the bonnet, legs splayed, arms outstretched; rain dripped from his black hair. He stared at me, his nose squashed against the windscreen, his wide eyes pleading for help. With exaggerated deliberation, the officer inspected Johannes's passbook, then shone a torch in his face.

'Waar is jou huis?' he asked.

'Number 1154, Mphuti Street, Officer.'

He turned to me, 'Why is this boy with you?'

'He is my garden-boy. I am not very familiar with the township and I asked him to show me the way.'

He stood to attention and saluted, 'Dankie Sister, all is in order. Okay Kaffir, you can go.'

A drenched Johannes climbed in the back and I started the engine. The wipers whipped across the windscreen, barely coping with the down-pour. Visibility was poor and the rain clattered on the thousands of shacks like stampeding wildebeest. And then it stopped. The sky lightened, the clouds floated away to let the sun through and just for a second its rays transformed the raindrops on the ugly tin roofs into a sea of shimmering diamonds. But it was only a mirage. The reality was before us.

Johannes leaned forward, 'We are here!' he shouted, and pointed to a shack on the roadside. 'There! Stop there.'

I couldn't believe what I was seeing. The dilapidated construction in front of me was just a metal box, possibly part of an old shipping container, with plastic and cardboard for windows. Johannes pushed the makeshift door open and with some trepidation we walked in.

Water dripped through the cracks in the roof and seeped up through the mud floor; the fetid smell of infection filled the air. Essie's whole body heaved. I tried to close my nostrils and not breathe. Johannes struck a match and lit the storm lantern I always kept in the car, 'She's over there,' he whispered, 'in that corner.'

The make-shift bed was raised off the floor with bricks; in the shadowy light I could just make out a bundle of blankets curled up on the mattress. It moaned and moved slightly. I swallowed hard. 'Essie, there's a plastic sheet in my bag, put it on the floor, there in the corner where it's dry. Johannes....'

'Sister?'

'You must pick up Nomano and bring her over here.' I dragged the mattress and blankets off the platform and placed them on the plastic. 'Put her there Johannes.'

Essie knelt beside the terrified girl, 'Don't worry,' she said, her voice calm and gentle, 'just lie still, you're going to be okay.'

I wasn't so confident. Nomano's right leg was so swollen it looked as if the skin would split and beads of perspiration gathered on her forehead and nose; she felt cold and clammy. I needed to examine the wound. 'What's this Johannes?' I asked, and pointed to a strip of something wrapped round her right calf, 'it looks like animal skin.'

'I do not know Sister. The Sangoma took out the bullet and gave her strong medicine to kill the pain and make her sleep. But I have no more to give her and she is not better.'

I looked around the filthy room, 'Johannes, who lives here?'

'No-one. A friend told me it was empty, so I thought it would be safe.'

'Is there a Primus stove?'

'Ja, I brought it from my place.'

'You must boil some water; I'll re-dress the wound, then we'll take her to the hospital.'

But an agitated Johannes had more bad news. 'Sister, the police have ordered all doctors to report any persons with bullet wounds. We cannot take her to that place.'

'The bullet has gone,' I said, sounding more confident than I felt. 'We'll say she caught her leg on a spike. Now you must run to the clinic and fetch one of the nurses. Tell them it's an emergency.'

After twenty long minutes the sturdy figure of Sister Thembu appeared, puffing and panting, her heaving chest stretching the buttons on her white uniform to the limit. She crouched beside the terrified girl.

'Molo Nomano. Unjani?' she said quietly.

'Molo Mama. I am well.' She attempted a smile, 'But my leg is very sore.'

'Ja, I see it Nomano.'

Sister Thembu turned to me, 'Annie, how can I help?'

'I've never seen this type of dressing Sister Thembu and I'm not sure what will be underneath.'

'It is traditional African muti, or medicine,' she explained. 'The Sangoma has used three layers. See this strip of goat's skin? It is strong and keeps the wound dry. I will cut this away. Now you can see the second layer; the agapanthus leaves act as an antiseptic and dampen inflammation.'

I watched carefully as she peeled away the broad green leaves to expose the final layer. A poultice of herbs covered the wound; it was crusted with blood and pus and crawling with wriggling grey maggots. Essie retched and disappeared out of the shack.

'Yes Annie,' Sister Thembu continued, 'this is good traditional muti.'

I was shocked by her comment - she was a respected qualified Nursing Sister.

'But this wound's infected, how can this be good medicine?'

Sister shook her head and sighed, 'It has not worked because the stupid Sangoma did not clean the blade. A good healer would not make this mistake.' She shrugged and paused, I could tell she was choosing her words carefully. 'You see Annie, sometimes the Sangoma's muti is all we have. If she gets better it is the will of the Spirits, if she dies it is her time.'

I was incensed. I wanted to find that witchdoctor, grab him by the neck and shake him till his teeth rattled.

'But this is Nomano we're talking about.'

She met my gaze, her eyes full of sad acceptance, 'I know Annie, I know.'

I had a lot to learn.

Turning my attention to the injury, I took a clean syringe from my bag, washed out the herbs and wild life with cool boiled water, then re-dressed the wound with sterile gauze and a cotton bandage. 'Sister Thembu, she needs antibiotics.'

'I agree Annie. I know the doctor at the hospital, he is Afrikaans and likes to drink, but he is a good man and will not ask questions. I will give you a note.'

It was now five-thirty and almost dark outside. I couldn't risk taking Johannes in case the police stopped me again; he would have to find his own way back. So, with Nomano on the back seat covered with blankets and Essie in the passenger seat, I drove through the shadows of the Township to the main road.

The approach to the hospital, an imposing Victorian building, was well lit. Of course, the front entrance was for Whites only. And the Blacks? We followed the signs pointing to the back of the building.

There was just one dim light over the entrance. A sign on the door warned: *Slegs Swartes ... Blacks Only* and a metal sign ordered, *Ring and Wait*. Essie looked at me and pushed the metal bell. We could hear it ringing somewhere inside. A few minutes later the door swung open and we half carried, half dragged the whimpering Nomano into the waiting-room.

I looked around. The room was all metal; metal bars at the windows, metal benches screwed to the floor and a metal water dispenser... no cups, just a sign that said, *Out of Order.* A strong smell of carbolic invaded the stuffy atmosphere and faded posters, encouraging vaccination against TB, decorated the grubby grey walls. It was more like a prison than an emergency medical facility. At the far end of the room another door and another notice, *Ring and Wait.* Essie pushed the bell, then we sat on the cold hard benches and waited. I looked round at the other casualties.

One young man groaned and clutched his side, a bicycle spoke sticking out of it. Another man with a jagged head wound tried to stop the trickle of blood with his fingers. I offered him some gauze squares. He smiled and took them.

'Dankie Sister, thank you'.

The room exuded despair and resignation. I had never been in the 'black section' of a hospital before and I wanted to take Nomano and run. But where to? Eventually an ageing black nurse appeared in a white uniform with burgundy epaulettes, denoting her rank of Sister. 'White people are not allowed in here,' she said quietly.

I answered just as quietly, 'I have a note from Sister Thembu for Dr van der Merwe and I'm not going anywhere until this patient is seen.'

Completely ignoring Nomano she took the note and disappeared. Five minutes later we were ushered into a small treatment room. Of course we would jump the queue! I was a white European - in a Sister's uniform.

The Doctor, dressed in green theatre scrubs, stank of beer and cigarettes. He spoke English with a strong Afrikaans accent, 'Sister, put her on the table then I will attend to this wound. You can wait outside.' Was Nomano invisible? I wondered.

'Thank you, Doctor, but we'll stay.'

He shrugged and growled, 'Just don't get in my way.'

The concept of a sterile environment was a joke, no masks or gloves, but at least he washed his hands before he removed the dressing.

We all peered in. Essie swayed, her face ashen, but she managed to stay upright.

'Another bloody witchdoctor's mess,' he sneered. 'I'll clean it out properly and give her a Penicillin shot. You can bring her back in a week.'

Nomano lay deadly still, eyes tightly shut. Essie and I stood on either side of her; she squeezed our hands hard 'Ayee, uncedo, uncedo,' she wailed, calling to her ancestral spirits for help. But despite my misgivings the Doctor did a competent job.

'I've finished now Sister,' he said, 'perhaps you will apply the bandage?'

But *I* hadn't finished, 'Dr van der Merwe, the penicillin?'

His eyes flickered, 'Yes Sister.' Clearly irritated, he grabbed a phial and a needle and syringe, drew up the dose and jabbed it into her thigh. Then, making no effort to conceal his sarcasm, drawled, 'Is that all, Sister?'

I met his gaze and shook my head, 'I think she'll need a course of oral antibiotics.'

Taking a deep breath, he pressed his narrow lips tightly together, walked over to the medicine cabinet and removed a plastic tub. Very deliberately he counted out fifteen tablets. 'One, three times a day, for five days,' he snapped, shrugging out of his gown. 'You can take her now.' He strode over to the stainless-steel sink and turned on the tap.

'Where can I find a wheelchair?' I asked. Even with his back to me his disdain at my persistence was palpable.

'There are none.' Then something must have nudged his conscience. Perhaps it was my contempt? 'A moment Sister,' he said, 'we'll keep her overnight. The ward is outside, across the passage-way.'

Essie and I made our way down the dim corridor, supporting the traumatised girl between us. Once outside we could see the lights of the ward block. A nurse met us at the door, she looked at Nomano, who was almost in a state of collapse, and shook her head. 'Sister, Doctor van der Merwe knows I have only thirty beds and fifty-two patients, where must I put her? No, you must take her with you. It will be better at your place than here. She will die if you leave her here.'

I glanced down the ward, every bed and space were occupied; patients in beds, patients on mattresses between the beds, patients perched on chairs. The stench and noise were unbearable. I thought about my spotless ward at the clinic and knew I couldn't leave her in this overcrowded, understaffed ward.

We struggled back to the car and I switched on the two-way radio, 'David?'

He answered straight away, 'Yes Annie?'

'Nomano is injured, I'm bringing her home.'

'Okay. If you think it's the right thing to do. Over and out.'

He was waiting outside as we arrived at the house and picked up Nomano as if she were a feather. 'Where must I put her?' he asked.

'She can stay in the guest room, the bed's made up.'

'You sure Annie? You know it is against the law.'

'I'm sure.' It wasn't the right time for a discussion, but I knew there would be words later.

Essie and I slumped on the veranda, exhausted and shocked by the lack of humanity. 'You must go now,' I said, 'if there's any trouble you mustn't be involved. We can manage.'

But she wouldn't hear of it. 'No Annie, I'm here to help, you might need someone who speaks Afrikaans.'

Two hours later an exhausted Johannes turned up. He'd hitched a ride for most of the way and walked the rest; he was determined to help look after Nomano.

That night we took turns to sponge her down with tepid water to try to reduce her temperature. We offered sips of fluid and gave her paracetamol, but in the morning, despite all our efforts, her temperature was even higher. In desperation I called a doctor I knew who I was sure would be sympathetic and discreet. He arrived with a drip-set, intravenous antibiotics and stronger pain killers.

'It's touch and go Annie,' he said, 'she has septicaemia. The next twenty-four hours are crucial, but you really need to move her out of the house to her own room. You know the rules.'

'As soon as there's an improvement,' I promised.

Johannes never left Nomano's side and over the next ten days she slowly recovered. But David, always a stickler for rules and regulations, was worried.

'Annie, we'll be in terrible trouble if someone reports us to the authorities. We shouldn't be looking after her in our house and you know it is against the law for Johannes to stay over-night. Apparently, there have been spot checks by the police in this area; they are targeting domestic servants who are allowing their boyfriends to stay.'

I knew he was right and promised to talk to her. But Nomano had already made the decision to leave. That evening she came to the kitchen, 'Annie, tomorrow Johannes will take me to Pretoria where we will stay with friends until I am well. But before I go I will fetch a good girl to look after you.' She grinned at me, 'And then I must go to see the

Sangoma. If you had taken me back to him,' she admonished, 'he would have made me better much quicker.' Clearly, she hadn't lost her sense of humour!

The following afternoon she appeared in the kitchen, a rather large toothless lady in tow. 'This is my friend Martha,' she announced. 'Her English is poor and she is very old, but she will work hard for you while I am away *and* she will find you a *very* good gardener.'

Fishing in her pocket she produced a small bottle of cloudy liquid and pressed it into my hand. 'I have been to see the Sangoma, I told him you have been married for a long time, but still no babas. He was very sorry to hear that and offered to help you.'

I was astounded, I was only twenty-nine and babies were certainly not on my agenda!

'The Sangoma says if you drink this, ten drops every day until it is finished, you will have many children. This is my gift to you, with my thanks.'

I dipped my finger in the muti... it tasted remarkably like Epsom salts!

And so, Martha stayed. She was so quiet and respectful we scarcely knew she was there, and that suited David. As for the new garden boy, Willie, he was just as ancient and hardly knew a weed from a flower, but was pleasant enough and always helpful.

But the place wasn't the same without Nomano. When David was away there was no noisy political discussion around the kitchen table. No wild lewd dancing to Miriam Makeba's song, *Pata Pata*, which meant, according to Nomano, *touch touch!*

Martha brought the occasional message from Nomano; the latest said that she and Johannes would not be returning to Johannesburg. And Essie? No newspaper would print her story, so she moved to Cape Town.

David and I realised that the experience with Nomano and Johannes had proved to be quite traumatic, and we agreed that politics should be off the agenda. He loved his job and I enjoyed working at a private clinic in Johannesburg, despite the fact that it was for Whites only.

Gradually we slotted into the comfortable South African lifestyle of barbecues, swimming and tennis. But there was another world out there in the townships and to give me an insight into how the majority of black people lived, I joined a local charity as a nurse volunteer.

It was a time of uncertainty and unrest. Across the country the sporadic acts of terrorism increased and the police and army were on high alert. There seemed to be a permanent air of anxiety; safety was often the topic of conversation. The latest fashion was for white women to carry designer guns and attend afternoon 'gun-parties'.

Target practice usually took place on immaculate lawns, between cups of tea or gin and tonics, where they were taught how to handle weapons and shoot to kill. My colleagues tried to persuade me to carry a gun, or at least learn how to shoot, but David and I decided that violence was not for us; we both knew we could never kill anyone.

But when terror came it was devastating.

It was exactly quarter-to-seven in the morning when we felt the blast. I was in the admissions unit with Lori, an Afrikaans nurse, ready to hand over to the day shift. The building shuddered, windows rattled, and black smoke diffused the sun. Terror panicked the city into setting off a cacophony of sirens, alarms and whistles. An explosion at the railway station, just a few hundred yards from the clinic, had derailed a packed commuter train from Soweto. Lori and I joined a team of volunteers to set up triage points.

The huge steam engine lay twisted on the track, like a giant work-horse panting its last breath. Fire-hoses trained on the obsolete wooden carriages and there was an overwhelming stench of burning. The platform was full of bodies; the dead and the injured. Terrified commuters ran, screaming, trying to get to the exit. Others wandered about aimlessly, numb with shock.

A terrified child clung to me as I carried her to the safety of a waiting ambulance. But the response from the medic was as shocking as unexpected. 'Sister we can't take her. She must go in the other ambulance to Baragwanath Hospital in Soweto - it is just for black people.'

The reality of apartheid lay in my arms. I hadn't noticed she was black.

I was incensed, especially when I realised that triage in this complicated country did not mean assessing *medical need,* it meant separating *Blacks* from *Whites*, and the *insured* from the *uninsured.*

I rang David, 'I'm going to be late home, I'll explain later.'

'That's okay Annie, take your time. By the way, have you remembered I'm going up to Mozambique tonight? You're off-duty for four nights, why don't you come with me?'

'I like the sound of that. Okay, see you later.' I'd fill him in with the details when I got home.

He was waiting on the stoep when I arrived, 'We have a problem,' he said, his expression grave, 'come.' I followed him to Martha's room. Nomano sat on the floor under the window, Johannes stood next to her; they looked exhausted and dishevelled. I instinctively knew they were somehow involved in the train disaster.

'Were you there Nomano?' I asked.

Her eyes filled with tears, 'Yes,' she whispered, 'but it was not meant to be like that. The bomb should have gone off on the track before the train arrived, then no-one would have been hurt.'

Her naivety was breath-taking.

'Nomano, violence is never the answer. Did you not learn anything from when you were shot? Do you understand that if you are caught they will hang you?'

She looked at Johannes. He nodded, as if he knew what she was going to say.

'Yes Annie, I know. But this is our fight. We deserve a better life.'

'What will you do now?' I asked.

'We need to get to Mozambique. We have friends in the Movement there who will help us get to Rhodesia, but we have missed the transport. They will wait for us over the border at Komatipoort, but for only for twenty-four hours. We must be there by tomorrow morning.'

Johannes butted in, 'Mevrou Annie, we are in a lot of trouble. Somehow the police have our names and we could not think of anyone else who could help us.' He glanced at David, 'Meneer David has said he will take us across the border.'

'But this is the last time Johannes, you're putting all of us in danger. I'll take you because I believe you didn't mean to harm anyone. I don't think the border guards will stop me, they know me well, but then you're on your own.'

Johannes held out his hand and took David's in his, 'Baie dankie, thank you. You are a very good man Meneer David. We will never forget your kindness.'

I couldn't believe my law-abiding husband was doing this, but ....

The journey to the border took just over eight hours and for most of the journey Johannes and Nomano hid under blankets and boxes in the back of the Land Rover. There was little to say.

We arrived at the border as it opened. It was six o'clock and the early morning sun cast a subdued orange glow through the haze. The sleepy guard saluted David and raised the barrier

'Have a good trip Sir,' he said, smiling, 'you too Mevrou.'

With a sigh of relief, we drove across to the Mozambique border control.

Another barrier, another uniformed officer. After taking a cursory glance at our passports he waved us through. We were finally safe.

Johannes had instructions to meet their contact at a village about two miles down the main Lourenco Marque's highway. There was no other traffic on the road and we soon spotted the small group of thatched rondavels set back among a copse of wattle trees. David pulled over. 'This must be it Johannes.'

A few moments later a man appeared from behind the trees and walked slowly towards the driver's door. David wound the window down, 'You are?' he asked the man quietly.

'Moses.'

'You are looking for?'

'Johannes and Nomano.'

Johannes jumped out of the back of the car, followed by Nomano. 'Ja man, we are here.'

'Come,' I heard Moses say, 'we are ready to move.'

Nomano leaned into the cab of the Land Rover and took my face in her hands, 'I cannot say all my thanks Annie. Our life *will* change.' Her eyes full of tears, she added, 'And it will be better. From here we are going into Rhodesia, but we will be back.'

We watched as they followed Moses to a waiting truck and scrambled in the back. The driver switched the headlights on, revved the engine and they were gone.

Dawn was breaking as we picked up the coastal road that would take us to the fishing village of Xai Xai then inland to the Limpopo National Park and the Research Station. We didn't say much, both of us relieved the journey had been without incident and Johannes and Nomano were safe, or as safe as they could be.

In many places the bush had taken over; wild mango groves and banana fronds encroached onto the narrow road, which in places was just a potholed track with concrete strips. David had travelled this route many times, but we were exhausted, emotionally and physically, and progress was slow.

An hour later we stopped at a road-side stall. A notice scribbled on a cardboard box made David laugh, which broke our thoughtful silence. He read it out loud in an exaggerated accent, *porquinho-mealheiro, Obrigado,* that's Portuguese for money-box, or piggy-bank, I think!'

We picked up a couple of out-of-date bottles of Fanta Orange, a carton of Portuguese cigarettes and two ripe fat mangos, then dropped twenty rands in the honesty box.

'Nomano said our lives would change,' David mused. 'She said that Africa does that to people. She was right Annie, our lives will change. We've a lot to think about.'

'Do we want to stay in South Africa? Can we deal with the political situation?' I asked. The answer was 'Yes' to both questions, but I was astounded when David told me he was going to join Helen Suzman MP and her Progressive party.

'I listened to her message to the country Annie. She said, "I stand for simple justice, equal opportunities and human rights", and it really resonated with me.' He looked at me, 'If we are going to stay in this country then we must do what we can to support human rights. But, Annie, we must stick to the rules and stay within the law.'

'I know, but what made you change your mind about politics?'

'It was soon after Nomano came to work for us. I was giving her a lift to the bus when a white policeman stopped me and said she wasn't allowed to sit in the front seat, she must either sit in the back or walk. Don't you remember? Of course, Nomano chose to walk. It made me realise what an unjust society we are living in.' He paused, 'And that's another reason why I offered them a lift to Mozambique.'

'Looks like we're reading from the same page at last,' I joked. But I knew he was serious.

True to his word, David became an active member of the Progressive Party and I joined the Black Sash Movement, a group of professional women supporting human rights for all.

Two months later a message arrived from Nomano, via Martha.

We are now safe and well in Rhodesia. We cannot thank you enough for all your help. Perhaps one day we will meet again, hamba kakuhle umhlobo wam, go well my friends.

Epilogue

Following the bomb incident, the headlines read;

> "LOOTERS RAID DERAILED TRAIN AT JOHANNESBURG STATION."

There was no mention of a bomb, and the reported numbers of dead and injured were wildly inaccurate.

David immersed himself in his research, but civil war had broken out in Mozambique and the research station relocated to a section of the Olifants river, south of Phalaborwa, on the edge of the Kruger National Park. Annie decided to join him. She gave up her job at the private hospital, swapped her bright red Volkswagen beetle for a more practical Jeep and went to work for a Non-Governmental Organisation supporting refugees fleeing from Mozambique.

Martha and Willie, who proved to be honest and loyal, stayed on to look after the house.

And Steve Biko? In 1977 He was arrested at a police road-block and died in police custody, age thirty.

Dispossessed

She stands alone beside the smouldering walls,
a silhouette against a flame-licked sky.
Her dreams lie scorched and drift on acrid sands,
her mind absorbs the war through bitter eyes.

At night she walks barefoot on desert trails
and humming to an ancient air creates
an unseen dance of soulful, careless grace
that lulls her raging thoughts of vengeful hate.

War-wearied but with faith unbowed, she joins
in hope nomadic streams of rootless tribes
and to her shrunken milk-less breasts she binds
with love a starving child. And on she strides.

As willing hands take up her precious load
with grateful thanks she whispers, 'God is good.'

The Fractured Halo

*When someone rape you
tell your mam or your
friends because you
will die or you will
found the AIDS or
you will become
pregnant*

.... *anon*

I was used to death. Every Saturday the burial bus, weighed down with hymn-singing, prayer-chanting mourners, lurched down the road towards the ever-expanding graveyard. No trees, no flowers or grass grew on the kopje, just a thousand wooden crosses hammered into the stony ground delivering the same message, *Rest in Peace*. How could anyone rest there?

And now my mother Thembeke Mdake aged 32, God Rest Her Soul, lies in a wooden box strapped to the roof of that bus, while I must sit in the front seat squashed next to the Pastor and take her to that dark place where the sun's soft rays will never touch her face.

For months I'd taken my mother to the hospital, now I must take her for the last time. Not for treatment, it was too late for that, but for a signed form saying she would die soon and may be entitled to a social grant. We both knew she was fading. We both knew I needed her to tell me who and where my father was and we both knew she would never see the promised brick house with running taps, electric lights and a flushing toilet.

No. My mother would die here in this shack, where the tin roof flaunts the sparkling frost in winter and takes hostage the stifling heat in summer; where the floor morphs into mud and mosquitos when it rains, and the gaps and cracks welcome the wind. But she had known no other.

The ambulance would not enter this Township, so I wrapped my mother in blankets and pushed her borrowed wheelchair over the rutted tracks to the road, where the Pastor waited with his bakkie to take us to the hospital.

Together we hoisted the chair onto the back of the truck then unceremoniously hauled my mother up. I lay next to her on the floor and held her in my arms, while the Pastor drove the four miles to the dreaded Department of Sexual Medicine for Women.

The entrance, hidden at the back of the concrete building, displayed a faded sign, *Blacks Only* - a reminder of the apartheid days. But only Blacks came here anyway, even poor Whites went elsewhere.

A long, dreary corridor led to an airless waiting room, where the sickly smell of disease and disinfectant crept over me, urging me to retch. I was not patient. I watched the clock on the wall and read the posters; *Abstain, Be Faithful, Condomise*, and *Women against Rape*. I counted the heap of free condoms that no one took and placed them in neat piles, then did it again. Nine o'clock, ten o'clock. Still we waited.

I walked up and down, up and down, while my mother led other patients in prayer.

'Zukisa,' praise God, she chanted.

'Siyancoma,' we are praising, they responded.

'Zukisa Njalo,' praise God every time, my mother urged.

'Siyathandza,' we are praying, chanted the patients.

At exactly 11.55am the consulting room door opened and the clinic Sister came out; smart in her white uniform with burgundy epaulettes, she oozed efficiency.

'Mrs Thembeke Mdake?' she called.

The safety valve in my head released its steam, 'Yes Sister, this is she,' I snapped, and wheeled her into the room.

A black doctor in a white coat sat in judgement, 'Stand,' he demanded. 'Take off her clothes.'

I sensed my mother's helpless resignation; she was too sick to care.

His face curled with distaste at her grey parchment skin and sagging breasts as he watched the Sister weigh her bones, for there was no flesh. From his swivel-chair he inspected her; up and down, back and front, then stretched his well-fed belly across the polished desk, pressed his stethoscope to her skeletal ribs and listened to her shallow breaths. In-out, in-out.

'She has the grant,' he pronounced.

My whole being raged against this man's inhumanity, my mother's selfish God, this rainbow nation. There was no black or even brown in my rainbow and no gold at its end, just poverty and violence. My mother placed a warning hand on my arm and with quiet dignity she thanked this man who did not deserve her thanks.

But I could not stop my venomous tongue, 'I see none of Mandela's Ubuntu here.' I spat.

My anger and despair was reflected in the Sister's eyes. 'Come kleintjie,' she said, 'let me help you.'

So together we dressed my dying mother and I took her home.

Later that evening I heard her voice from behind the curtain that separated our beds, 'Sindiswa come. Sit by me.'

'I am here. I am listening,'

'Sindiswa, I must tell you how it was.'

So, I lit the Primus stove, pulled a blanket round my shoulders and sat beside her on the bed. She reached out and took my hand.

Her voice shook as she started to tell me the story I had been waiting to hear.

'It was the winter of nineteen-ninety, my 16th birthday, the age you are now Sindiswa, and the year Tata Madiba Mandela was released from Robben Island. That day I will never forget; every detail is burned into my brain.

'I was late for the community centre where I helped at the crèche. As I ran down the track I could see my friend Tomas on the corner setting up his stall; sun ripened mangos, cabbages, squawking chickens scrapping in a cage, and sheep's heads which he roasted over hot coals until the mouths stretched taut into evil smiles. Sometimes he would let me poke in the eye sockets, searching for the sweet brains inside, then I would suck the soft creamy meat off my fingers. I liked Tomas.

'When he saw me he waved, so I skipped across the street towards him and asked him if he had some fruit for me as it was my birthday. I remember how he laughed. He picked me up and swung me round and round until I was dizzy, then gave me a noisy kiss and pressed a big fat orange in my hand. It was a good start to that day Sindiswa.'

'What was he like?' I asked.

'Oh, Tomas was coloured, not black like me. His skin was the colour of coffee with cream; he had silky black hair and when he laughed his dark almond eyes crinkled. He called me his black angel, he said my frizzy curls looked like a black halo.

'I think he really liked me, but he was married and I had promised to live by the Church's instruction, *Abstain and Live.* The teacher told me it meant that if I did not have sex I would not catch HIV/Aids and die. So I decided I would not do that thing until I was married.'

She paused and looked at me, 'you must also abide by this rule Sindiswa.'

'I promise Ma,' I replied.

Her voice was weak yet determined as she continued. 'The crèche was just a rusty old shipping-container inside a fenced compound. Every day we made food for at least two hundred orphans; we played games and sang songs, sometimes we worked in the vegetable garden. The hours always passed quickly.' She stopped and took a deep breath. She looked so sad.

I could see she was very tired and handed her a cup of Rooibos tea, 'Drink this Ma,' I urged, 'you will feel a little better.'

'Ayee Sindiswa, I remember every detail of that day,' she whispered. 'Now I must tell you that which is difficult to explain.'

Warming her hands around the cup she sipped the tea. 'It was five o'clock on that day and almost dark; it was my turn to lock up. I was ready to leave when I heard an engine in the yard, I wasn't expecting anyone so I peered out of the window. The headlights picked out the shapes and shadows of the compound and then I could see it was only Tomas in his bakkie. I was so relieved to see him that I rushed to open the door and waved to him. He waved back, "Hey Thembeke, how goes it?" he called.

'He came in and perched on the desk, swinging his long legs, just like he always did. He seemed his usual friendly self but then offered me a can of a beer. I didn't drink alcohol, but he was so persuasive I sipped a little, just to be polite. I asked him why he had not gone home; he told me he had brought me a present, but I must first give him a kiss. I laughed Sindiswa, thinking it was a joke, but then he grabbed my arm and pulled me towards him.'

I sensed her hesitation, 'Ma, you don't have to tell me this if it is too painful.'

'Yes, I must tell you everything, then you will not judge me.'

She continued, her voice soft and sad, 'I didn't like *this* Tomas and jumped away, but as I moved towards the door he stuck out his foot and I crashed to the floor. I felt my arm crack, it was so sore I thought it must be broken. I remember starting to cry and asking him why he had done that, but he just laughed.

'I was very afraid Sindiswa. I told him Pa was waiting for me by the Big Shop and if I was not there he would come to find me. But he just stood over me, staring. I was so scared. I remember sobbing and begging him to let me go. Even today when I close my eyes I can see his face and hear his words, "You are a woman now Thembeke," he said, "but not yet a real one."'

I put my arms around my mother's fragile body, 'No more, you must rest now.' I urged. But she was adamant.

'No, I will tell you, then I will rest.' And so I listened to that I did not want to hear.

'I watched him unfasten his belt, "Come my little black angel, I know you like me," he said. Then I knew what my present was to be. I did struggle Sindiswa and I screamed, but he was so strong, and anyway there was no-one to hear.' She paused, 'I felt his searching fingers and I gagged at the sickly smell of dagga and beer on his breath. And then strangely, in my fear, I felt calm.

'I remembered my teacher telling me that if I was ever attacked I must stay still. I must not struggle. But I must try to remember every detail so I could tell the police and they would catch that person. Then I bit my lips, dug my nails into my palms and lay still, frozen in watchfulness. I seemed to be outside my body, looking down, but that could not be. Could it Sindiswa?'

I couldn't stop my tears at her bewilderment, 'I don't know Ma, perhaps your spirit was with the God uQamata, and he was looking down on you, protecting you.'

She looked at me in surprise, as if she hadn't considered this, then nodded, 'Ayee Sindiswa, I think it was He.' She took a deep breath, 'When Tomas had finished with me he told me I should be grateful and I must not tell anyone or he would have to kill me.

'I heard his laugh as he climbed into the bakkie and started the engine. Through the thin curtains I saw the brightness of the headlights sweep around the compound, picking out the crèche and the toilet block, then he drove out of the gates. He was gone.'

I held my mother close, our tears mingling as I shared her sorrow, but still she carried on. 'My legs were shaking Sindiswa and my new skirt was torn; there was blood on it, I think it was from my hands. I was sore everywhere and my arm hung at a funny angle, but I managed to crawl to the door and lock it. Then I used all my strength to push the desk in front. A few minutes later the lights went out and it was black. I did not know what was happening until I remembered the generator clicked off at half past five.

'In less than half an hour Tomas had taken my life and my soul.

'There were no cell phones or land lines in Tshwane in those days, but I knew Pa would find me, so I crouched under the desk and waited. It seemed a long time had passed, then I heard Ma calling, "Thembeke, Thembeke," followed by Pa's deep voice, "Thembeke we are here." Somehow, I managed to open the door enough for them to squeeze through.

'Ma cradled me in her arms and wiped my tears, and hers, with her skirt. I could see the horror in Pa's eyes when he saw my ripped clothes and injured body, "Who did this to you Thembeke?" he asked. I told him it was Tomas from the food stall. He said I must tell the police, but I told him I could not as Tomas said he would kill me. Pa insisted, he said I must be brave and trust that the police would find him, so he could not do that thing to anyone else.

'The police came in a car. They said I must not be frightened, they would catch Tomas and send him to jail for a long time. They took me to the hospital where the doctors fixed my arm, then took my blood and swabs to test.

'The Sister said I could go home and return the next morning to attend the HIV/Aids clinic, but I would not go back there Sindiswa, it was for bad people. I turned my face to the wall and did not speak or eat or drink for a long time.

'When I knew I was with child I crawled away from that world to the kraal of my ancestors in the Transkei. Each day I worked on the land and at night I slept next to my grandmother, Gogo, in her hut. She made my food and gave me goat's blood mixed with milk to make me strong, and the Sangoma threw the bones and gave me medicine.

'And so Sindiswa, you were born in that place I was born, Umtata. The next day Gogo slaughtered a cow and we praised uQamata for your safe birth and beauty, your loud voice and strength. Your life gave me back my life.'

I broke the silence, 'Why did we have to come back to Tshwane?' I asked. 'Why did we not stay with Gogo? I know she wanted us to stay, I remember how she wept and wailed when we left.'

'I was very sick for a long time and I needed Gogo to help me. Every-day she would strap you to her back and take you to tend the fields and the goats. You grew sturdy and strong like a tree. She told you about our ancestral spirits and showed you how to make paint from plants and the red earth, to make pictures. Do you remember Sindiswa?'

'Yes, I remember. Gogo also told me about the bush and the animals and how the Tokolosh would bite off my toes if I was naughty, so I tried to put my bed on stones so those mischievous spirits wouldn't get me.'

Ma laughed, 'Do you remember when I would teach you our isiXhosa language? How you would get the click sounds in the wrong place and the word would turn out completely different?'

'You were a good and patient teacher Ma, and look how well I learned.' Her tired eyes lit up, I could tell she was enjoying those memories.

She paused in thought, then continued. 'We came back Sindiswa, because I wanted you to go to a better school, where you would learn to read and write and find out all about the world. You were four years old when Oupa came to fetch us. We lived with him and Ouma here in this shack in Tshwane Township, until they both got sick and passed over. Then there was just you and me.'

We fell into a comfortable silence.

After a while she carried on reminiscing. 'Do you remember Sindiswa how you hated being inside that school? You cried so much for Gogo that the teacher gave me work so I could be near you.'

'I remember the uniform, that ugly brown pinafore dress, white blouse and black shoes; how I hated those shoes ... I was so used to running bare-foot. And do you remember Mevrou Barnard? She was sooo strict, and after school finished on Fridays she made us clean the classroom ready for Monday, even the windows.

'But it was good you were there Ma. I remember singing as we walked that long road to school together; how you would dance in the long grass, twirling and whirling, stomping and chanting. And you would tell me about life.'

'Ja Sindiswa, they were good days. But I was always worried you would also have the HIV, so I asked the Doctor to test you.'

'I remember going to the hospital,' I replied, 'when the doctor took my blood and I cried. I was so frightened of the big needle.'

'Yes my child, but uQamata protected you and you did not have the virus. Look at you now Sindiswa, you are sixteen years old, a beautiful young woman. You have passed the matric, now you can go to college and be a teacher or a lawyer. You have been a good daughter.' She paused again, her breaths now rapid and shallow, her black face grey with pain. But she would not rest.

'I would have liked to have had a good husband and a father for you Sindiswa, but I found the HIV had slithered unseen into my body and snaked spitefully through my veins. Then I knew I could never lie with another man. Slowly it attacked every part of me until I became very sick, but the doctor said I was not sick enough for medicines.' She looked at me, 'How could that be Sindiswa?'

I shook my head in despair, 'I do not know. It was very wicked.'

The hiss of the Primus stove filled a brief silence, then in a voice so soft I could barely hear, my exhausted mother whispered, 'Tomas was sent to prison for a long time. He died there from Aids. That is how it was. That is my truth.'

Eventually I spoke. 'He was my father.'

She nodded, 'Yes my child.'

'I remind you, every day, of him who did that to you.' I said.

My mother smiled, then held her hand out to touch my face; gently she stroked my cheek. 'No Sindiswa, I see my strong, beautiful daughter, you are not like him.'

I looked down at my skin, the colour of coffee with cream, and touched my straight silky black hair. I knew the truth and wished I never knew. Now I did not know who I was.

That night my mother slept in my arms. When I could no longer feel the warm wisps of her breath on my cheek, I wept.

Daylight brought the Pastor and church Elders to pray for her soul. Alone I washed her lifeless body, smoothed the halo of curls and dressed her in her blue Zionist robe. I placed her hands together in prayer and softly kissed her forehead, then watched the Elders put my precious mother in a wooden box and close the lid. She would stay with me in this shack for two days.

On Saturday the mourners would come and eat the meat of the slaughtered cow, chant and sing and praise the Lord. Then the burial bus would collect her and we would make our last journey together. But I would not praise that God.

After the burial I stayed with one of the church Elders. They said I must not stay by myself, the township was not safe for young women to be on their own. The next day I returned to the shack where I had spent twelve years of my life; robbers had taken everything, even my mother's clothes.

The church found a family to house me, but I would not stay there in Tshwane. That evening the children from the crèche brought gifts; two oranges, a beaded scarf made by my friend Elvira, a seed bracelet from the care centre, and a card signed by everyone.

In the morning I wrapped my belongings in a blanket, balanced it carefully on my head, as my mother taught me, and walked to the main road to wait for the bus.

The driver took my bundle, then climbed on the roof and squashed it between the piles of luggage, sacks of mealie-meal and sugar, and squawking chickens in cages.

The chattering passengers sat crammed together. A big fat Xhosa mama, her sleeping baby swaddled on her back, found me a space next to her,

'Come kleintjie,' she said, 'sit by me. Ek is Nolunthandu. What is your name? Where are you going?'

And so I took my mother's love, her strength and courage, and started the eight-hour journey to that place where I was born, Umtata.

The Car Jacker

Late in the dark September gloom
carjackers crouch with watchful greed.
Behind the thorn bush out of sight
their shadows wait, they wait to fight.

And when the unsuspecting prey,
with headlights bright, drives into view
and red lights warn that they must wait
until the green light shows the way

Then good friends chat and fail to see
the dangers lurking in the dark.
The engine slows, the brake lights flash,
the faceless pounce, the windows smash.

With greedy hands they grab their spoils,
and good friends scream and shield from
shards of glass and sharpened knives
their children, fearful for their lives.

Then from the dark night hope appears,
sirens scream and armed guards shoot.
The game is done, the robbers flee
and life is saved, the good friends free.

But then a fear so overwhelming
seeps through the very bones of life,
and guns and fences become the way
we live our lives, the price we pay.

And as we guard our precious world
our freedom slips away, we lose our soul.
And fearful thoughts keep trust at bay
the carjacker has won the day.

Spirit of Africa

He was there at the crossroads, standing apart from the rest. Men waiting to be picked up for work, men drunk at eight o'clock begging for a few cents, women selling flowers, kids selling newspapers. But he wasn't begging or selling, he was just there, watching.

There was a certain nonchalance about him. A black hoody hung on his tall skeleton-thin body; he wore ripped jeans and laceless trainers, a black rucksack slung over one shoulder.

Becca watched him as he leaned against a street light. He reminded her of a Masai warrior, indolent and graceful; she sensed his every muscle, nerve and sinew poised ready for flight. His profile revealed sculpted cheek bones framing a slim face and a slender neck which looked too fragile to support his perfectly shaped head.

She tingled with excitement; her fingers itched to grab a pencil and sketch him.

He knew she was watching him and changed his stance.

The lights turned to green and he started to walk away, unhurried yet purposeful, but not before she'd caught a glimpse of an upturned mouth grinning in acknowledgement. On a whim, she reached into the cool bag on the passenger seat, pulled out a bottle of water and wound the window down. 'Hey,' she shouted, 'catch,' and tossed the bottle towards him. It flew in a perfect arc. He looked around, casually reached out his arm, and with the grace and skill of an athlete, caught it.

Behind her the impatient cars edged forward, beeping horns, until the cacophony of sound was overwhelming. She didn't care, they could wait. She caught his grateful smile as with one swift movement he unscrewed the lid, gulped down every drop and tossed the empty into the bushes, then with a cheeky wave swaggered off down the highway. She thought about him all day.

The art teacher stood over Becca's shoulder and watched as she drew sketch after sketch, discarding each one until the waste bin was overflowing, unable to capture that elusive something. 'Perhaps he would sit for the class?' she suggested. 'We could pay him a small sum, and he probably needs the money.'

But she didn't want to share him. She wanted him to sit only for her. Her mind raced ahead. He could be my project, she mused, the title could be *The Dedicated Gardener*. I would call him Amahle - Xhosa for *The Beautiful One,* and spend days sketching him. She carried on dreaming; perhaps a series of paintings in different mediums? Amahle, burnished by the sun, leaning on a spade. Amahle in action; digging trenches, mowing the lawns, dead-heading the flowers.

The possibilities were endless, but how was she to persuade him to sit for her? Then she got it! The answer was obvious. She thumped the air, 'Of course! Pa will give him work in his garden centre.'

The following Wednesday Becca left the house at seven-thirty in the morning, as usual; the electric gates swished closed behind her. As she turned onto the road she could still hear her Mom's strident voice shouting from the open window, 'Becca, don't forget what I said.'

As if she would! She knew the mantra off by heart, "Don't stop for anyone, not even an accident. Keep your car in gear, don't wind your window down, keep the doors and windows locked, don't give to beggars, don't buy anything from road-side sellers, and don't talk to strangers."

'Yes Mom,' she muttered under her breath, 'and what would you say if you knew I was about to proposition a stranger? Especially one hanging around on the street corner.'

Becca stopped just before the crossroads and pulled onto the grass verge. Her eyes swept the road ahead; he was there on the central reservation. He saw her. She wound the window down and smiled. With three long strides he dodged the traffic and peered into the car. 'Morning Miss,' he said and grinned, his sparkling white teeth shocking against the blackness of his skin.

She could feel her cheeks burning. He was so beautiful; dark oval eyes with the longest lashes, lips not full but generous and firm. 'Surely, I'm not blushing,' she thought, 'What would he think?'

Not knowing quite what to say she stretched over to the passenger seat, grabbed her lunch and offered him her cheese sandwich and a bottle of water. 'Here! I thought you might want this.'

He unwrapped the sandwich and took a bite, then another, his tongue licking stray crumbs from his chin, his eyes never leaving hers until he had finished. Then his face crinkled into a smile,

'Thanks, I needed that, I didn't have time for breakfast this morning.'

Mmmm, a sense of humour too, Becca thought, then turned to the matter in hand, trying to sound efficient, 'I see you every Wednesday at these crossroads, are you looking for work?'

'Ja. I can do anything; gardening, cleaning...' his voice trailed off. He looked directly at her, his eyes serious, his tone personal, 'I would like to work for you.'

Is he flirting with me? She wondered.

'First things first,' she said, stifling an urge to smile, 'what's your name?'

'Nelson.'

She laughed, 'As in Mandela?'

He grinned, 'Ja, my mother has his picture on the wall, but *my* name is Nelson Debeza.'

'Okay Nelson Debeza, do you know Mulders Drift?'

'I do.'

'My Pa is looking for workers; he runs the garden centre there. Can you be there by eight o'clock on Friday?'

'Yes, dankie. I'll be there.'

'I'll tell him to look out for you. Ask for Meneer van Niekerk and tell him Becca sent you.' She fished in her bag, pulled out a business card and scribbled her name on it. 'You can give him this,' handing him the card, 'and remember, eight o'clock sharp, he likes people to be on time.' She wanted to add, *and I want you to get the job,* but thought better of it and drove off.

The first part of her master plan now accomplished, she just had to persuade her father to employ him; he wouldn't be happy with her for not checking with him *before* she asked Nelson... but!

Stuart van Niekerk, Becca's father, glanced down at the note his daughter had left on the hall table.

Hey Pa, Sorry I missed you earlier. I'm staying at Carla's tonight, but I've something really exciting to tell you, so I'll call you in the morning, or you could ring me later.

xx Becca xx.

He chuckled to himself. She was up to something, but he had more important things on his mind.

Stuart van Niekerk was a man of great routines; every Wednesday evening, without fail, he would put the dustbin in front of the gate ready for collection on Thursday morning.

But a couple of weeks ago he'd noticed that some of the rubbish had been strewn about the pavement. Something or someone had been attacking his bin!

'I'm determined to catch the culprit, Elspeth,' he told his wife, 'I'm going to keep watch behind the fence. I'll catch whoever, or whatever is doing this.'

So, at ten o'clock that night, Stuart filled a flask with coffee, placed a sun-lounger behind the hedge and waited.

It was nothing new for him, he loved sleeping outdoors, especially in the spring when the air was pleasantly warm, the sky peppered with stars and Tessa, his arthritic German shepherd, to guard him. Well, at least keep him company.

It was six o'clock in the morning when the culprit came. Tessa growled. He put his hand on her head, 'Quiet Tess,' and moved closer to the gate. He watched as a young man walked towards the house. He looked to be in his early twenties; tall and slim he wore a black hoody, ripped jeans and a woolly hat pulled down over his ears.

As he approached the gate he looked around, checking there was no-one about, then pulled the lid off the bin and stood back. The black flies swarmed out, grateful to be free, and his arms disappeared into the buzzing rubbish. After fishing around for a few seconds, he finally emerged with half a loaf of bread, a couple of over ripe peaches and a jar of ... something, stuffed them in his rucksack and sauntered off down the road.

Stuart had felt uncomfortable; the boy was obviously poor and hungry, but what could *he* do? He wanted to talk to him, but didn't know what to say and didn't want to frighten him away. What do you say to someone rifling through your dustbin? he wondered, and what could I do about his poverty? What would I achieve if I gave everything I had to the poor? I would just end up poor myself. The thoughts whirled round in his head. Perhaps I could offer him work in my garden centre? But then again, I know nothing about him.

So, he did nothing.

But all that day Stuart found himself thinking about his dustbin thief. What if Becca was in that position? Would he want someone to help her? He made a decision.

The following week he placed fresh food wrapped in cling-film on top of the rubbish; bread and cheese, a piece of fruit, a can of coke. In fact, whatever he'd been able find in the fridge and whatever his wife wouldn't miss. He knew she wouldn't approve.

Sure enough the young man was there again. His face lit up when he saw the food parcel. He peered up and down the street, then with a smile and a nod picked it up and nonchalantly walked off.

Stuart sat on the stoep sipping a cold beer, pondering over the recent events. It was Wednesday again and he still wasn't sure what to do about his dustbin thief. He took Becca's note from his pocket and looked at her scribbled message, she was his only child, indulged and privileged. This boy had nothing. Then he knew what he had to do, he must try to help this young man.

'Sorry Becca,' he muttered to himself, 'whatever it is you want will have to wait until tomorrow, it's time to put the dustbin out!'

Once again Stuart placed a food parcel inside the bin, but this time he left a nearly-new blue hoody in a plastic bag, one that didn't fit him anymore. Then, with the faithful Tessa beside him and a flask of strong coffee, he settled down on the lounger and waited.

At six o'clock the following morning the boy arrived. He seemed different, confident. Stuart could hear him laughing and talking to himself as he punched the air, 'Ja man, dankie, but I might not need your charity for much longer, I think I'm going to get work.' Then stuffing his old black hoody in his rucksack, he pushed his arms through the new blue one and strode down the road munching an apple.

Stuart smiled to himself, yes, it was the right thing to do.

An hour later, after a quick shower and a mug of Rooibos tea, he climbed in his bakkie and drove to the garden centre.

He was checking the order books in the office when the phone rang. 'Van Niekerk speaking.'

'Pa, it's me.'

'Yes Becca. I got your note and have been expecting your call. What is it that's so exciting? I'm busy.'

'Pa, I know you're looking for workers, well I think I've found you one.' She gabbled on, 'His name's Nelson. I told him to be at the garden centre at eight o'clock on Friday morning, that's tomorrow, is that okay?'

Stuart sighed. He would do anything for his daughter but he wished she wouldn't interfere in his business. This was the third time she'd asked him to hire someone. 'I think you should leave things to me Becca, the last two workers you recommended were charming and good-looking, but useless.'

'But Pa!'

Stuart, resigned to the inevitable, gave in. 'Okay, but this is the last time.'

'Yissss! Thanks Pa, you won't regret it.'

'Mmmm. But Becca, he must have some identification and preferably a reference.'

It was seven o'clock on Friday morning when Stuart turned onto the Rustenburg Rd, heading towards Mulders Drift. Becca's latest protégé was expected at eight o'clock.

He watched the boy stride into the yard, bang on time; he immediately recognised the blue hoody. It was him! *The dustbin thief.* 'Goeie more, good morning,' Stuart called, 'can I help you?'

The young man walked towards him, twirling a woolly hat in his hands. He held out a card, 'Goeie more Meneer,' he said politely, 'I am looking for Meneer van Niekerk.'

'Well now you've found him! What can I do for you?'

'I am Nelson Debeza. Your daughter gave me your card, she said you are looking for workers and I must be here at eight o'clock. I can do gardening or any other work; I am strong and a very good worker.'

'How old are you Nelson? Where're you from?'

'I am twenty-two years old and come from Port Elizabeth. I passed the matric but could not find work, so I came to Johannesburg.' He shrugged, 'But there is no work here either, so I have been doing anything to make a few rands.

'My pa was a farmer so I know the land, then my friend said that the people in Rand Park Ridge can afford to pay a gardener, so I came there. In the evenings I play saxophone in a township band.'

'Have you papers and a reference Nelson?'

He fumbled in his rucksack and pulled out a creased envelope. 'Yes Sir, I have a reference from a lady in Rand Park Ridge. I worked in her garden for six months, but she's gone to Durban to stay and the new owners did not want me.'

Stuart scrutinised the letter:

To whom it may concern. Nelson Debeza has worked for me for six months. He is reliable, a good worker and is honest and helpful. I can recommend him for garden work and other odd jobs. It was signed *Mrs E Opperman.*

'Yes, I know Rand Park Ridge,' he murmured.

He also knew the Oppermans and that Nelson was telling the truth. 'Do you have an ID card Nelson?'

'Yes Sir,' and handed it over.

'Okay Nelson. Everything seems in order so I'll give you a two-week trial, starting tomorrow. Do you need a place to stay?'

'Yes Sir. I have nowhere. I've been staying in the township with a friend, but I had to sleep on the floor.' He laughed, 'That family is very big, there are many, many children. Sometimes I slept in the yard, sometimes in the bush.'

'Then fetch your things, there's a room here. Piet, the foreman, will show you round and explain everything; he'll give you boots and overalls. Meals will be provided during the week, pay day is Friday at twelve mid-day and you'll have Saturday afternoon and Sunday off. Does that sound fair?'

Nelson's face lit up, 'That sounds very fair Meneer, thank you. Perhaps I can start today?'

'Ja, Ja. That's okay.'

The following day Stuart was about to leave for the garden centre when he heard Becca calling, 'Pa, wait, I'm coming with.' She flew down the path, long blonde hair streaming behind her, a brown leather satchel on her shoulder and a small portable easel under her arm.

'You do know it's Saturday?' he joked.

She giggled, 'I know Pa, but I've lots of work to do. I'm going to sketch Nelson.'

'Nelson will be working, he won't have time for you.'

'It's okay Pa, I'll just sketch while he works. I won't interfere.'

Stuart shook his head, 'Some hope!'

Becca walked across the yard to the overgrown field where Nelson was working. He was in the long grass, stripped to the waist and wielding a scythe; his body moving with ease - rhythmical and strong.

'Morning Nelson,' she called.

He looked up, a slow smile spreading across his face, 'Morning Miss.'

'My name's Becca.'

'Ja, I know. Okay Becca, what brings you out here?'

'I'm an art student working on a project for my final exams. I decided to put together a collection of paintings in different mediums, using the garden centre for inspiration. I think you'd make an excellent model.'

'Have you decided what to call this project Becca?'

'Well, I was going to call it *The Dedicated Gardener*, but when I thought about it, it's not about one gardener and the soil, it's about all the people of Africa who are the gardeners of life. Digging out the strangling weeds and sowing seeds of hope; dealing with adversity and moving forward; forgiving the past and becoming one united nation.

'I want to capture that spirit by portraying different aspects of life; working on the land, resting, playing, living life.' She wanted to say 'loving', but instead found herself blushing again - and tongue-tied.

'Wow Becca! That's some deep philosophical challenge,' he said, grinning, 'and as you got me the job how can I refuse?'

Every day she followed him around, observing him while he worked; her sketch-pad filled rapidly. They were almost inseparable; took breaks together, shared food and drinks, went to the beach and cinema, and would chat about everything under the sun.

Becca knew her father liked Nelson, but her Mom certainly didn't approve of her spending time with him. She still lived in the past when apartheid ruled and Blacks and Whites didn't, or rather were not allowed to mix. But Becca didn't care, she sensed a real spark between them. Then one evening, as they sat on the river bank watching the huge orange sun slowly dip into the water, he gently turned her face to his and kissed her.

'I think I love you Becca van Niekerk.'

Elspeth van Niekerk was not happy with her daughter's blossoming relationship with Nelson.

Finally, she voiced her concerns to her husband. 'It's been six months since Nelson started working for you Stuart, and Becca spends so much time with him I rarely see her these days. It's not right.

'She insists there's nothing in it, that she's just sketching him for her art project! She says as it's her final year and the tutors like what she's doing, I should leave her alone. So, I did. But earlier this evening I saw them down by the river holding hands, they were completely oblivious to anyone or anything, obviously a couple.'

Stuart sighed, 'They are serious Elspeth. They're talking of a future together, perhaps marriage. He's a good boy, honest and intelligent, I like him. I think he'll be an asset to the centre, he has some great ideas and adores Becca. Life's different now,' he continued, 'it's good to see the young folk mixing, and before you say anything, she loves him. Why don't you give him a chance?'

'No Stuart,' she said firmly, 'it will never happen.'

'I think you're wrong Elspeth and I would rather you didn't say anything to Becca. Try to see it from her point of view.'

But the following evening after dinner Elspeth cornered her daughter. 'Becca, I know you're fond of Nelson and I can see he's a nice boy, but I hope you're not thinking of marrying him. It wouldn't be right.'

'And why is that Mom?' she asked, tight lipped.

'Well, he's not like us. He's Xhosa and he's black.'

It was the wrong thing to say.

'You're living in the past Mom,' Becca replied, her voice an icy calm. 'Apartheid's finished. We're a rainbow nation and I can marry who I like. You should accept that I'm a grown woman and make my own decisions. And just to be clear, Nelson's not a *boy*, he's twenty-two years old, an adult.'

But Elspeth couldn't let it go. 'What about HIV and AIDS? So many people have it. And what about children? What would they be like? What colour would they be? What would our friends and neighbours say? And have you thought about your grand-parents? It would kill them!'

Becca glared at her mother; stony-faced, eyes narrowed.

'*We*,' she said, '*We* are responsible people. We have both been tested for HIV, as the Health Department recommends. It's available and free to everyone, as is the advice on safe relationships. And our children, if we are lucky enough to have any, will be beautiful and loved.

'I won't give him up Mom and until you're ready to accept that, I'll be staying at the garden centre.'

Becca stormed off to look for her father; she found him in the garden puffing on a cigarette. By now the tears were flowing, 'I know it's hard for Mom,' she sobbed, 'she's so old-fashioned when it comes to mixed-race relationships. If only she'd give Nelson a chance. You've accepted him Pa. You welcomed the end of apartheid, but then you've always treated everyone as equal and you always find something good in people. But I won't give him up.'

Stuart shrugged his broad shoulders and put his arm round his angry daughter. 'It is as it is Becca. She's lived with apartheid all her life. Be patient, give her time and try to carry on as normal, she'll come around eventually. I hope you're going to carry on taking us to the bowling club on Fridays, at least that way we can all keep in touch.'

'Sure Pa, I'll be there, but tell her I won't discuss Nelson.'

It was one o'clock on Friday afternoon when Becca dropped her Mom and Pa at the club; clear blue skies and a gentle breeze meant a perfect day for bowling. But night falls fast in Africa and at eight o'clock when they left the club-house it was already dark. There were no street lights, just trees and scrubland on either side, but Becca knew the road well and there was very little traffic.

Elspeth sat in the passenger seat clutching her handbag, relaxed after her two large glasses of Cape Sauvignon Blanc, while Stuart lolled in the back-seat singing along to the radio. His deep voice, fuelled by Castle lager and whisky chasers, boomed out the old Jeremy Taylor song, *Ag Pleez Deddy*.

'Come Becca, join in,' he insisted.

And so they bowled along, singing the silly song at the tops of their voices.

Ten minutes later they approached the crossroads at Mulders Drift. Becca pulled into the middle lane, ready to carry straight on to Rand Park Ridge. The robots turned to amber, then red.

As she braked a car pulled up beside her, on the outside lane. The driver kept the engine revving, then pipped the horn and flashed his headlights. She turned to acknowledge him, thinking it must be someone who knew her.

He gesticulated wildly and pointed towards the inside lane, then wound his window down a fraction. 'Look!' he shouted, pointing to the roadside, 'GO, GO, GO,' then shot through the red lights and roared off down the highway.

'What on earth did he say?' Stuart muttered.

'I think he said, "Go, go," Becca replied and turned to look where the man had pointed.

At that moment the passenger window exploded, the noise reverberated round the car. Becca heard her mother scream; she watched, mesmerised, as a gloved hand pushed through the fragmented glass and grabbed hold of the bag on Elspeth's lap.

He pulled, she tugged. She wouldn't let go.

'Get the gun Becca,' she screamed, 'it's in the glove compartment.'

The hand tried to get to the catch to open the door, but Elspeth stabbed at it repeatedly with a piece of broken glass. 'Becca, get the gun,' she shouted again.

Stuart, now roused from his happy stupor, joined in the shouting, but he couldn't do anything from the back seat and Becca couldn't reach the glove compartment. The radio continued to blast out more verses of the irreverent song.

'Give him the bleddy bag Elspeth,' Stuart roared, 'just give it to him woman and shut that bleddy stupid song off.'

'Mom, let him have the bag,' Becca pleaded, then yelled, 'just give him the bag!'

'Drive off Becca,' Elspeth screamed, 'put your foot down! Go through the lights.'

Becca released the handbrake and pressed her foot down on the accelerator; as the car started to move the man on the passenger side let go of the bag and ran off into the bushes, empty handed.

It was then she noticed a second man, running towards the driver's door. In one swift movement he struck the window with small hard object; the glass shattered into a thousand pieces. Becca screamed. Luckily the toughened safety glass held most of the pieces together, but in the chaos she let go of the wheel and stalled the engine.

A hand punched through the shards of glass and reached for the keys. Becca tried to grab his sleeve, but he pulled away and it caught in the jagged edges. In the desperate attempt to free his arm the hood came off, exposing a black face and close-cropped hair. For one awful second, she thought it was Nelson.

The face stared at her, then past her. His eyes widened in horror. She turned her head and saw Elspeth raise her arm and take aim. 'Nooo,' she shrieked. Too late.

Everything seemed to happen in slow motion. Becca saw the flash and heard the bang. It was almost surreal. A moments silence... then the screams from the terrified man filled the car as the bullet smashed into his shoulder.

She watched in horror as he desperately tried unzip the hoody and wriggle out of it, but it was firmly hooked on the glass. A dark stain of blood seeped through the material then dripped down his shirt and onto Becca's jeans. She wanted to help him, but couldn't move; she seemed frozen to the seat. Finally he succeeded, and clutching his injured arm ran across the central reservation into the bushes.

The bloodied hoody dangled from the smashed window. No-one spoke or moved. Cars sped past, no-one willing to stop. Of course they wouldn't!

A few minutes later they heard a siren. Becca put the hazard lights on and sounded the horn. A police car slewed across the junction and screeched to a halt. Stuart ran towards it, 'Help, help,' he shouted, frantically waving his arms, 'over here. We've been attacked.'

The car doors flew open and three policemen carrying assault rifles jumped out. The sergeant, a short stubby man, approached the car, 'We had a call to say there was an attempted smash-and- grab. You folks okay?'

Becca nodded, too shocked to speak.

He turned to Elspeth, who was still holding the revolver, 'And you Mevrou?'

'I shot him Officer,' she said, quite calmly, although her white face and shaking hands told otherwise. 'I think I got him in the shoulder, but then he ran off.'

'Good shot Mevrou,' he said, with inappropriate admiration. 'Lucky you had a firearm with you, but I think you'd better give me the gun.' Without a word Elspeth handed it over. 'We'll need this for evidence,' the officer continued, 'but don't worry, you'll get it back, it was clearly self-defence. This road has become quite popular for car-jacking and smash-and-grab. You're lucky we got here so quickly, we were actually on our way to an accident when the call came through.'

He turned to Stuart who was now standing beside the car. 'There's a lot of blood about Sir, is anyone hurt?'

Stuart shook his head, 'No Officer, the blood belongs to that bleddy thief.'

He turned to Becca, 'How about you Miss?'

'No, just a few scratches, we'll clean them up when we get home.'

'Okay. Then I must ask you to go to the police station and give a statement. It's not far, through the lights for about half a mile then take the second turning on the left.'

'You mean we must drive this car Officer?' Stuart asked in disbelief.

'Yes Sir, if you leave it here it'll be stripped down to the frame by the time the insurers come to collect it.

'I'll take the hoody as evidence.'

'What about the man Mom shot?' Becca asked.

'Ag don't worry about him, he'll probably turn up at the hospital. They probably used spark plugs to smash the windows, it always seems to work. Before you go I'll knock the windows out completely, it's safer than driving with shattered glass. Sorry we can't escort you, it's a busy night.'

Stuart stared at the policeman in disbelief as he started to knock the remaining broken glass out with the butt of his rifle. The advice usually given by the police was, *always drive with your windows closed and the doors locked,* and now, although the doors might still lock, they had no windows!

The police station was off the main highway, down an unlit road and inside a compound. A few suspect-looking men hung around the perimeter fence, some obviously drunk, others injured. Elspeth didn't want to get out of the car, but Stuart insisted they all went in together.

It was clear that the officer was not the least bit interested. She stood behind the desk noisily chewing gum, one hand resting on the leather holster at her hip; she looked about sixteen.

'Yes?' she asked.

'We've come to report a smash-and-grab,' Stuart said. 'The traffic police told us to come here; we need a reference number.'

Without looking up the officer pushed a note-pad and pen across the desk,

'Just put your details on the top sheet, then I'll take a statement. I doubt whether we'll find out who did it, you're the fifth today.'

'But I shot one of them and injured his shoulder.' Elspeth said in a low voice.

'No problem, I'm sure he deserved it.'

Between them they described the events while the young policewoman wrote it down. 'Did you recognise the man, Sir?' she asked.

Elspeth jumped in, 'Yes Officer, I think it was a young man, Nelson, who's been working for my husband. He looked just like him *and* he wore the same blue hoody. Yes, I'm sure it was him.'

'Mom,' Becca shouted.' How could you? It wasn't him. I should know.'

The Officer turned to Pa, 'Did you recognise him Sir?'

'No, I'm afraid I didn't.'

'Do you know where Nelson stays, Sir?'

'Yes, he stays by my garden centre at Mulders Drift. His name is Nelson Debeza. I can call him on the cell phone.'

'That's okay Sir, I'd rather you didn't do that. We'll check it out and let you know, but you should get an HIV test, your thief seems to have lost a lot of blood.'

The interview was over in 15 minutes.

Stuart insisted on driving home, despite being over the drink-driving limit. He drove fast and furious; he didn't stop, not even for red lights. Becca sat in the passenger seat urging him to slow down, but he ignored her.

From the back-seat Elspeth tried to explain why she had mentioned Nelson's name. 'Blacks all look the same to me Becca. He wore the same sort of hoody as Nelson and we were near Mulders Drift. I'm sure it was him.'

'Leave it mom, I'll call Nelson on his cell phone.' There was no reply.

They sat up late into the night drinking coffee laced with brandy. 'Good for shock,' Elspeth said.

Stuart slumped in a chair, ashen-faced. He looked across at his wife. 'You have to stop this nonsense Elspeth. You could have killed that young man, whoever he is. The law says innocent until proven guilty and that is right and proper. Tomorrow you must tell the police you no longer want a gun and they can dispose of it.'

But Elspeth had to have the last word 'It's a good thing I had it,' she said, her voice smug and self-righteous, 'we could all have been dead.' And with that disappeared to bed, convinced her actions were vindicated.

It was after midnight when the phone rang. Becca answered. 'Yes?'

'Miss van Niekerk?' the voice asked.

'Yes.'

'This is Inspector van Zyl, Mulders Drift Police. That boy of yours, Nelson. He hasn't been shot, he's very much alive and well. We found him in the barn carving an impala out of a piece of wood and very good it was too. You needn't worry about your mom, there's enough evidence to show it was self-defence, and anyway we may never find him.'

'They won't find him,' Becca said, after she'd put the phone down, 'they won't even look for him.'

But the following day the Inspector rang again to say a man with a gun-shot wound had been picked up by a patrol car and taken to hospital. 'It was probably the suspect,' he said, 'but forensics will check the blood on the car and the hoody; he's sure to be sent down for a long time.'

Despite Stuart's insistence that they should carry on as normal, the incident proved to be life-changing for everyone. Security measures at the house and Mulders Drift were tightened and Stuart and Elspeth stopped socialising after the match at the bowling club; they only played in the early afternoon so they would be home before nightfall.

Elspeth was charged with the attempted murder of Zolani Ndega, the man the patrol car picked up. It was an open and shut case. Ndega pleaded guilty. The Judge ruled self-defence and Elspeth was acquitted, just as the policeman had predicted.

But despite her protestations that Ndega deserved to be shot, Elspeth found it difficult to come to terms with the fact that she almost killed someone, so she handed her gun in to the police.

And Becca?

Fear overwhelmed her. She didn't drive with the windows down. She didn't stop at red lights, even if the road was clear, and she never drove at night without someone with her. That someone was usually Nelson; they were inseparable.

Stuart let them move into the offices above the garden centre and helped them convert the space into a lovely apartment. He also allowed them to use the barn as a studio for Becca's art work and Nelson's carvings.

But Elspeth was determined she wouldn't accept Nelson. She rarely went to Mulders Drift and Becca no longer took them to the club. Despite desperately missing her daughter she still felt that mixed relationships were morally, if not legally wrong and wouldn't change her mind about Nelson.

It was one Wednesday afternoon, almost twelve months after the car-jacking, that the call came. Elspeth dashed into the hall and picked up the receiver. 'Hello. Elspeth van Niekerk speaking.'

A very quiet, hesitant voice replied. 'Mom?'

'Becca?' Elspeth started to cry.

'Mom, it's my graduation next week. I've been awarded a first-class honours degree and won a scholarship to continue studying. My work will be exhibited in the university and then in the municipal art gallery. Please come. Pa's coming,' she hesitated, 'Nelson will be there.'

Elspeth knew this was the defining moment, she wasn't going to mess it up this time. 'I'll be there Becca, I wouldn't miss it for anything.'

'What about Nelson?'

She blinked the tears away. 'It'll be okay Becca. I'm so sorry. I've been a foolish old woman.'

At the awards ceremony they all sat together; Stuart, uncomfortable in his Sunday best, Elspeth looking stylish in a pretty floral dress and high heels, then Becca and Nelson wearing jeans and t-shirts.

The night belonged to Becca. She'd changed the name of her project from *The Dedicated Gardener* to *Spirit of Africa.* It was a collection of six pieces of work; Nelson working on the land; Nelson striding out of the river, water dripping from his toned body; Nelson, head back, laughing, joyous; Nelson at his work-bench carving an elephant; Nelson asleep in the barn with Becca's little Jack Russell asleep on his chest. But the pièce de résistance was the stunning charcoal and ink drawing of Nelson playing his saxophone. This last piece was given a special award; the critics were unanimous, she had captured his soul - Nelson *was* the Spirit of Africa.

The frames too received recognition. Nelson had hand-made each one and carved the title of the drawing round the edges in English and Xhosa. A local businessman was so impressed with his talent that he offered him space in his art shop to sell his work and take commissions.

That evening Stuart and Elspeth drove down to Mulders Drift; Becca and Nelson had invited them to share a celebratory barbecue. The evening went well; rib-eye steak grilled to perfection on an open fire, served with mealies and salads and followed by home-made pumpkin pie.

Becca gave her mom a guided tour of the apartment. The colour scheme reflected her love of the bushveld; ochre and turquoise, the pink shades of the protea and the vibrant blue and yellow of the strelitzias.

'It's beautiful Becca,' Elspeth whispered. 'I'm so proud of you.'

Later Nelson entertained them with his saxophone, playing traditional jazz; Becca sang some of Miriam Makeba's music and Stuart joined in with his old favourites - patriotic Boer songs. It was just like old times.

They got up to leave about ten o'clock. Becca, clearly happy that the evening had gone so well, hugged her mom as if she'd never let her go.

Nelson shook Stuart's hand, then looked directly at Elspeth. He smiled and held out his hand. She hesitated, just for a second, then took it.

'Are you okay Elspeth?' Stuart asked as they drove home, 'you're very quiet.'

'Yes, I'm fine. Just thinking what a wonderful day its been. I so enjoyed the evening with Becca *and* Nelson. You know Stuart,' she added softly, 'I've never shaken a black man's hand before. It felt just like mine.'

The Township Line

*The clickety clack
of the train on the track,
and the tippety tap
of the heels of the girls
in their skirts as they trip
to the station.
And the click of the tongue
of the Xhosa man*

*And the whoosh of the steam
from the train on the track,
and the noise of the boys
as they chat on the train
as it leaves for the shacks
in the Township.
And the click of the tongue
of the Xhosa man.*

*And the screech of the brakes
from the train on the track,
and the clunk of the doors
of the train as they slam
as it stops at the end
of the Township line.
And the click of the tongue
of the Xhosa man.*

All Roads Lead to Alfonso's

Nina forced herself to concentrate. Tired and a little anxious, she was beginning to wonder whether her friends and family had been right. "I strongly recommend that you and Sam re-think this idea Nina," her father had warned. "I know it's your honeymoon, but there is a war going on in Mozambique."

Of course they'd known about the war; it had been rumbling on for three years. It was 1964 when the *Front for the Liberation* of *Mozambique,* FRELIMO, sought to overthrow the Portuguese administration, but apparently the problems were mainly further north, or so they'd been told, and Vilanculos was still a popular destination for sailing, fishing and scuba diving, not to mention the amazing marine life.

The journey from Johannesburg had been uneventful; the roads were generally good and there was very little traffic. They hadn't seen any sign of military action, just a couple of Rhodesian helicopters flying north and the South African army on patrol at the border. But once they'd crossed into Mozambique and picked up the coastal road, the conditions were far from ideal. The bush had almost taken over in parts and the sandy pot-holed road, interspersed with concrete strips, was difficult to negotiate in the campervan.

The road suddenly bent sharply to the left; Nina slammed on the brakes, a massive tree trunk straddled the road. 'Oh no!' she muttered, 'not now.' She leaned across and nudged her snoring husband slouched in the passenger seat. 'Hey Sam! Wake up, we've got a problem.'

Sam opened his eyes and looked through the windscreen at the fallen tree. 'Blast! How far are we from Vilanculos?'

'About sixty miles I reckon and we're already a day behind the others.' She opened the cab door, 'I don't think we can go round it, the vegetation looks too dense on both sides, let's see if we can move it.' But despite their best efforts it wouldn't budge. 'What about using the van to tow the tree off the road?' Nina suggested.

'We could, but I don't really want to unless absolutely necessary, I'd rather not risk damaging it.' He looked around, 'Look, it's almost four o'clock, we'll lose the light in a couple of hours and I don't fancy driving in the dark. The chances of another car passing now are slim, but we could camp here for the night and make an early start. I noticed a small clearing back there, I think it was big enough to park the van, and there are bound to be some folk passing in the morning.'

Nina reversed the bright orange VW campervan to where the road widened. On the side of the road a flattened grassy area formed a rough semi-circle, certainly wide enough for the van, and it was evident from the traces of tyre tracks, discarded cans of beer and soft drinks, that vehicles regularly stopped there.

'I think this'll do,' Sam said, 'we'll set up camp then have a look round. According to the map the Olifants river must be somewhere near.'

A cup of coffee later and the intrepid pair set off to explore. About a hundred yards down the track they spotted a narrow trail leading down a steep slope, 'Careful Sam it's slippery here,' Nina called, as she lost her footing and slithered down the bank. 'We must be near the river, I think I can hear a waterfall - I can see it now, over to the left. What I'd give for a swim.' Then as an afterthought added, 'Hope there are no crocs!'

Through the trees they could see the river as it rushed and tumbled over a small weir, then swirled round a loose circle of huge smooth rocks, leaving behind a natural lagoon before meandering on to the Indian Ocean.

'There's our swimming pool!' Nina said, 'I'm in first, I need to cool off.'

Sam suddenly stopped, 'Nina! Look.'

He took her hand, guiding her to a gap in the undergrowth,

'Look there,' and pointed downstream.

They stood entranced as the scene unfolded, it was clearly the village wash-day! A group of women on the river bank, some bare breasted, others with babies strapped to their backs, rubbed and scrubbed the laundry, their firm strong bodies swinging backwards and forwards in a steady rhythm.

They could hear the *slap slap* of wet sheets on the sun-baked rocks as two slender teenage girls, chattering and laughing, whacked them on the stones. Then, hitching up their colourful capulanas, they stepped into the river to rinse the sheets in the flowing water.

It was clearly a well-rehearsed system; the dripping sheets were passed to a wizened old woman, who, with a skilful flick of her wrist, tossed one end to the outstretched hands of a heavily pregnant young woman. One by one they twisted the dripping sheets; squeezing, turning, squeezing, until the last drop of water spilled onto the bank, then with satisfied faces they spread them on the hot stones to dry in the sunshine.

Some of the washing was already dry and one big mamma, wearing a green and red striped voluminous skirt and matching head cover, gathered it up into a large bundle and placed it on her head. Then, with her considerable hips swaying and rolling, she clambered up the river bank, passed her bundle to waiting hands and returned for more.

In the safety of the lagoon a group of naked children splashed and played; the sun's rays catching the dancing droplets of water on their burnished skin, creating fleeting rainbows. Then it was their turn to be washed!

The determined mammas grabbed each wriggling child in turn, smeared soft brown mud over their sturdy brown bodies, then rinsed it off by dunking them in the water, before they ran laughing through the shallows.

They must have watched for at least half an hour when Sam suddenly put his hand over his nose and mouth,

'Oh no! I'm going to sneeze,' he whispered, desperately trying to stifle it.

But it was no good. His whole body convulsed as he let out an explosive *aaa-tishoo*, followed by another and another.

In seconds the mammas had collected all the washing, rounded up the children and vanished into the undergrowth.

Sam put his arm round his new wife and hugged her, 'Wow Nina! That tree trunk did us a favour, I wouldn't have missed that for anything.'

Nina scrambled down the bank, 'Couldn't agree more. Come on, last one in the water cooks the sausages.'

'Shouldn't we go and get our swimming gear?' Sam asked, with a lascivious wink, 'or are we skinny dipping?'

'Oh! I don't think so. You know my motto,' she said, returning the wink, *Be Prepare*d!' Then, in a single provocative movement, she slipped off her T-shirt to reveal a pink gingham bikini top.

Sam watched open-mouthed as she gingerly tested the water with her toe,

'Nina, you look amazing! Hang on, I'm coming in, how's the temperature?'

'It's freezing,' she gasped and plunged straight into the crystal-clear waters of the lagoon.

A couple of hours later, wearing soft cotton pyjamas with the long pants tucked into suede desert boots to keep the goggas from biting their ankles, they watched the day draw to a close.

The huge red sun, streaked with indigo and orange, slowly sank below the trees until they were in complete blackness. Snapping his cigarette lighter open Sam lit the citronella candles to keep the mosquitos away. The soft yellow glow of the flickering lights threw eerie shadows through the trees, creating an unearthly atmosphere.

He picked up his guitar. The music floated through the darkness, merging with the sounds of the night; an owl hooting in the distance, the chorus of chirping cicadas, the crackle of branches snapping, as if someone or something was lurking in the bushes, and the yelping of a jackal calling his family.

Nina relaxed into her chair, drinking in the atmosphere of the bush and reflecting on the day. She scribbled in her diary; *what an adventure and what a privilege to have witnessed such a delightful and innocent snapshot of African village life.*

A slight rustle in the acacia bushes warned them they were not alone. It was followed by two childish voices, giggling.

'Sam, I think we have guests,' Nina whispered. He grinned and nodded, then carried on strumming and singing. A few minutes later two small figures, holding hands, appeared from the gloom. Two little girls dressed in shorts and T-shirts; their skins almost as black as the night, eyes wide with excitement. They had to be twins, they looked identical, but one was just a fraction taller.

Nina smiled, 'It's ok,' she said and beckoned to them to come forward. Two responding smiles beamed back. The taller girl pointed to the guitar.

'Do you want to play?' Sam asked, not knowing if they understood English. They both inched forward, arms outstretched pointing to the guitar, clearly itching to touch it. Their eyes fixed on Sam. He nodded encouragement, then pointed to himself, 'My name is Sam,' he said, then pointed to his wife, 'and this is Nina.'

The girls copied his introduction. The taller girl pointed to herself, 'I Maria,' then to the other child, 'She my sister, Sofia.'

Sam placed the guitar on the ground 'Hello Maria and Sofia, do you want to play my guitar?'

The excited pair dashed across and sat beside it cross-legged; four small hands reached out to touch the strings, *twang, twang.* They plucked gently at first, then louder, **twang, twang.** Laughing with delight at the sounds they ran their fingers up and down the fretboard; plucking, strumming, tapping on the wood - making a rhythm from a melee of notes.

Maria leaned forward, she looked at Sam then picked up the guitar and placed it on her lap, touching and stroking it, then turned to Sofia and whispered in her ear. The two girls jumped to their feet, giggling. 'We sing,' Sofia announced, pretending to strum, and in sweet high voices they began to sing, in English, that well-known hymn, *Jesus Wants Me for a Sunbeam.*

They'd just started the second verse when a voice calling from the direction of the river, floated through the trees, 'Mareeea, Sofeeea.'

'Mama!' Maria gasped, and placing the guitar on the ground she grabbed Sofia's hand. In seconds they'd melted into the darkness, as if they'd never been there.

'How amazing was that,' Nina said, her voice low, 'and where did they learn to speak English and *that* song?'

'Probably the church. I think Mozambique's mainly a Christian country, Catholicism would have been introduced here by the Portuguese.'

They sat together in a comfortable silence under an inky-blue sky now peppered with stars and watched a full moon rise slowly above the canopy of trees.

Sam was the first to make a move, 'Come on Nina, let's turn in. We've a long day tomorrow.'

A sharp knock on the side of the camper-van woke the sleeping pair. 'What time is it?' a startled Sam asked.

Nina glanced at her watch, 'Half-past five.'

Pulling on a pair of shorts he peered through the cab window, 'Good God! Get dressed Nina, it's the army!' He opened the door a fraction, 'Who's there?'

'Captain Jose Mendes, Mozambique army,' came the reply, in perfect English. 'Could I have a word, sir?'

Sam stepped out. The van was surrounded by soldiers in camouflage fatigues.

'Is there a problem?'

'No, no problem. I wondered if everything was okay, it's an unusual time and place for tourists to stop. I assume you are tourists?'

Nina appeared in the doorway, now dressed in navy shorts and a white shirt, her unruly red hair tumbling round her shoulders.

'Good-morning sir. Yes. We're heading for Vilanculos where we're joining a flotilla, but there's a tree across the road, round the bend. We couldn't move it so decided to camp here, hoping that someone would come along to help us, or we could try to move it with the van.'

'Then you're in luck! We're heading that way. I'll get my men to move it. If you can be ready in half an hour you can join the convoy, it'll be safer for you.' He turned to the waiting soldiers, 'Okay. Sergeant Pereira,' he called.

A broad-shouldered soldier stepped forward and saluted, 'Yes, Capitan!'

'There's a fallen tree trunk ahead, clear the road and wait for me to join you.'

'Yes, Sir.'

Nina stepped forward, 'We really appreciate your help Captain Mendes, it won't take us long to pack up.'

'Please, call me Joe my mother does, she's English, It's my father who's Portuguese.'

Within fifteen minutes the awning was down and everything stowed away; the smell of coffee wafted from inside the van

'Time for a cuppa Joe?' Nina asked.

Chatting amiably while sipping the steaming coffee, Joe explained that the platoon was heading for Beira, which was much further north. 'I can take you to within twenty miles of Vilanculos, but where are you meeting the rest of the crew?'

'We've been told to head for Alfonso's Taverna.' Sam replied.

The captain laughed. 'Everyone knows that all roads lead to Alfonso's! He's famous for his seafood stew, hottest you'll ever taste. Wash that down with a few cold beers followed by a swim and a snooze on the beach. Fantastic! There's not much to do there you know,' he added, 'it's a very quiet place.'

'Actually, we're on honeymoon,' Nina explained. 'It's been our dream to sail round the Bazaruto archipelago, so we've arranged to meet up with friends then join a flotilla. We'll anchor off Santa Carolina for a few days and spend some time with old friends of my parents. They run a deep-sea fishing business there; we're hoping to fish for marlin.'

'Sounds good to me. Okay! I'd better re-join my men, you slot in behind the second jeep.'

The convoy of five jeeps and two supply trucks trundled off down the narrow road. An hour and a half later it stopped at a crossroads. 'This is where we part company,' Joe said, shaking their hands. 'You take the right-hand fork, we go left. Just carry straight on for about thirty-five miles; the road's not bad from here so you should be in Vilanculos in less than an hour. Safe journey and good luck.'

Nina took over the driving. 'We've been lucky so far Sam. Did you hear the helicopter overhead earlier?'

'Yes. Joe said it was just routine surveillance; the rebels are much further north. He said we shouldn't have a problem, but just to be vigilant and make sure we travel in convoy on the way back.'

Gradually the road widened and at last there were signs of village life; small kraals with pigs and hens jostling for space; farmers tending patches of maize and sugar cane, and women balancing piles of driftwood precariously on their heads.

The concrete strips became a sandy road; it wound round a small banana plantation to reveal a panoramic view of the Indian Ocean. Lapis lazuli blue, it stretched towards the islands of the archipelago before merging with the hazy horizon. 'Just look at that view Sam, it's stunning, and look.' Nina pointed to a weathered wooden sign at the side of the road, *Welcome to Vilanculos.* She stopped the van, 'Come on Sam,' and hand-in-hand they walked towards the beach.

A soft breeze carried the sounds and smells of the ocean; they could taste the salt on their lips and hear the screech of the seabirds circling the shoreline. Swaying palm trees and silver sands edged with yellowing dunes led down to the water's edge. The coral reef curved round, cradling an exquisite sparkling sea, and lace foam crests topped the urgent waves as they rolled to shore.

Mesmerised, they gazed in awe as two dolphins, leaping and twisting, showed off their skills. A silver shoal of fish darted through the shallows, shimmering in the reflected sunlight, oblivious to the hawk-eyed fish eagle ready to swoop.

'This is unbelievable Sam. I've never seen anywhere as beautiful.'

'I know, it's all been worth it. Come on, let's find Alfonso's.'

'That's easy,' she replied, pointing to a bright blue sign shaped like an arrow. 'That's the way to *Alfonso's Taverna,*' she declared triumphantly. 'Follow that arrow!'

With Sam now in the driver's seat the camper-van trundled up the cliff path. They could see the taverna ahead; the white stuccoed building, two storeys high with a red tiled roof, stood on a slight rise overlooking the ocean. As they drove up they were greeted by a group of children shouting and laughing, clearly fascinated by the bright orange vehicle. 'Hello, Hello! You stay at Alfonso's?' one of the boys yelled, 'I take you there. You wanna go fishing? My father got a good boat, very cheap!'

Nina laughed as another little boy ran alongside, 'I like your house. Can I have a ride?' he shouted.

A rather large man with huge moustache and wearing a blue striped apron, emerged from the building, 'You must be Sam and Nina.' He held out his hand, 'I am Alfonso. Welcome. We've been expecting you. The others have gone down to the beach, they said to join them when you're settled.'

He pointed to a clearing behind the taverna, 'Park your van there. There's a toilet and shower in the wooden hut and I've bottled water for drinking. Set up camp then come across, I'm sure you're ready for food and a cool drink. There's matata on the menu, that's my own recipe of spicy fish stew, served with rice, and my wife's home-made bolo polona, I think you would call it potato cake, and of course salad and plenty of Portuguese wine.'

Nina laughed, 'Oh we've heard good things about your stew, it's been highly recommended.'

That evening they walked down to the beach to meet their friends. The seductive, smoky smell of barbecued fish and lemons hung in the atmosphere. 'Hey Nina,' someone called, 'fresh fish from the boatman for supper tonight and prawns cooked in piri-piri sauce, garlic and lemons. Hope you've brought the Castle lager.'

In the distance the flotilla, white sails flapping in the breeze, rode on the tide of an ever-changing sea; aquamarine through the spectrum to the purple-green shadows of the deep-water channels.

Later, as the sun slipped beneath the horizon and the moon reached out its silver tendrils, lighting the ocean like splintered diamonds, Sam picked up his guitar. 'This song's for you, Mrs Thomas.'

September Safari

Africa is waking, the bush veld stirring,
a dung beetle pushes his ball up hill.
Delicate gossamer entraps a grasshopper,
and the scavenging hyena searches for a kill.

Round the thatched roof boma, crazy looped jasmine
fight bougainvillea for space to breathe, and the
green-scaled boomslang hanging from the thorn bush
flicks out his tongue in venomous greed.

Narrow ochre dust tracks, brown seared grasses,
sun-burst gazanias reflect the promise of the day.
Stampeding wildebeest chasing the rain clouds;
the cheetah spots a zebra and targets his prey.

Down at the waterhole the tic-ridden warthog
laps up his fill while down on his knees
and over in the distance springing impala
flee from the leopard desperate for a feed.

Grey clouds gather above the savannah,
bringing hope to the rivers of September rains.
Tall dry grasses wave a whispering welcome
and the lazy old lion dusts off his mane.

*Dusk brings mosquitos down to the waterhole
waiting to share their malaria with glee.
Elephants trumpeting, tic birds foraging,
the hyena finds a carcass a lion left free.*

*The bush now is sleeping except for the insects,
buzzing and humming they emerge from the ground.
Flying ants swarming, shadow spiders scurrying
and an indigo sun slips silently down.*

What Price a Social Conscience?

I knew about the 'West Wing', the section of the Cape Town prison reserved for white political prisoners, dissidents, enemies of the state. It certainly wasn't on my 'to visit' list.

The phone call came at 4am. 'Sean?' a female voice whispered. I immediately recognised the voice, it was Nadine, the wife of my friend and colleague, Declan.

'Yes,' I answered. 'What is it? Are you okay?'

'You must get away. They have arrested Declan and the others.' The fear in her voice was almost tangible. This was serious.

'Thanks Nadine.' The call clicked off and I replaced the handset.

Louisa stirred. 'Sean?'

I looked down at her tousled hair, her cheeks flushed with sleep. 'That was Nadine. I have to go, they've got the others so I'll be next.'

Louisa knew exactly what the call meant. We had prepared for this day. She knew what to do.

I stood for a second at the nursery door and gazed at my twin boys snuggled together in one cot; I resolved that as soon as it was safe we would leave this complicated country and go back home to Ireland.

I put my arms around my beautiful wife and held her close, 'Take the kids and go to your mother's place,' I said, trying to sound reassuring and in control. 'And don't you worry, I'll be back soon.' A hug, a lingering kiss, and she passed me the small rucksack kept packed for an emergency. It contained basic essentials; money, passport and a change of clothes.

It was one of those black, black nights; there was no moon, just a thick bank of cloud. I'd parked the car around the back of the house out of sight; the petrol tank was full and would easily get me to the safe house fifty miles away. Confident I couldn't be seen I opened the gates, ran back to the car, and putting the gears into neutral, free-wheeled to the road.

The engine started first time, but before I could switch the lights on I was dazzled by the headlights of a car in front of me. In the darkness I hadn't noticed the black car parked on the grass verge. I glanced in the rear-view mirror - of course they'd covered all possibilities! A second car edged towards me and another set of beams flicked on. There was no point trying to hide, so I opened the car door, stepped out and put my hands above my head. A voice came over a loud speaker, 'Mr. O'Connell, you are surrounded. Do not try to run, there is no escape.' A stocky man, dressed in army khaki and flanked by two armed officers, walked towards me,

'Mr Sean O'Connell?' he said.

I could feel my stomach churning, 'Yes, that's me,' I replied, trying to keep calm.

'My name is Roux, Major Roux,' his accent thick and guttural. 'I am arresting you on the suspicion of being an enemy of the state. You will be taken to a police station where you will be questioned, and you will appear before the magistrate's court tomorrow. Would you please turn around and put your hands behind your back?' All very civilised, I thought, as one of the officers placed the handcuffs on my wrists and escorted me to the unmarked car. 'My officers will inform your wife,' the Major continued, 'you will be allowed to call her from the station and you may contact your solicitor.'

Of course they would inform her and at the same time pull the house to pieces searching for incriminating evidence. But we had long since gone underground with the operation and our equipment was safely stored in various places across the city. They would find nothing.

Unsurprisingly there was no police station, no lawyer and no contact with the outside world.

I was taken directly to a prison in Bloemfontein, about a three-hour drive from Johannesburg and interrogated, then again and again. I was told that I was being held under the new 'ninety-day detention without charge' act and they would inform my wife where I was being held.

There were accidents; a fall down the stairs, a beating by a fellow prisoner, followed by a spell in solitary and visiting rights withheld. But on the whole, I wasn't treated too badly; I had a cell to myself and was allowed my own clothes and belongings. Eventually, and only when the case was due to be heard, was I allowed a solicitor.

On the ninetieth day I was taken to court. The proceedings were a farce. Most of the dialogue was in Afrikaans, and although I could get by in a one to one conversation, the legal jargon was way above my head. In the end I was officially charged as an enemy of the state. Bail was refused and I was returned to prison to await trial.

The excessive media attention came as a complete surprise. The press named us 'The Irish Four', although I'm not sure we deserved such notoriety. We were not brave, selfless men like Mandela and Sisulu, who would give their lives for their cause, we were just four journalists. Four Irish lads from Belfast who decided to join in the struggle for human rights for all.

Declan and I had always been best friends. We'd lived in the same Belfast street, attended the same school and ended up at the same University, both reading journalism. Tom and Patrick were on the same course and we'd shared a house, so it was no surprise that after four years studying we decided we needed an adventure. South Africa would be our starting point.

Our intention was to have some fun in the sun, make a bit of money and travel around Africa for a year, then settle down back home in Ireland. But it didn't quite work out like that. We found the standard of living and quality of life we enjoyed in Africa was something we could only have dreamed about in Ireland. And so we stayed.

Our hard-earned degrees proved to be a sound investment and led to extremely well-paid jobs. Declan and I reported for the Guardian; Patrick and Tom for The Rand Daily Mail. Tom's girlfriend, Jane, came out from Ireland to join him, then Patrick met Tamara, an English girl living in Johannesburg. I met Louisa, an Afrikaans speaking teacher from the Free State. Eventually Declan settled down with

Nadine, a midwife at the Queen Victoria Hospital. And now, seven years later, we were all married with children and living in the affluent suburbs of Johannesburg.

When we first arrived in South Africa we knew very little about apartheid; life was to be enjoyed and politics were not on our agenda. In fact, our mantra was, *no work and all play*. With hindsight we were naïve in assuming that apartheid would have little impact on our personal lives. The reality was so very different. Apartheid was everywhere and we just couldn't ignore it. Anyway, I had always had a social conscience and couldn't disguise my feelings about such a legal and considered abuse of human rights.

I suppose I was a little surprised when I was approached by Richard, a black colleague and ANC activist, who worked in the print shop. He asked if I would help him write a leaflet advertising an anti-apartheid rally and perhaps photocopy a few. Of course I agreed, and after discussing it with Declan we decided to offer our journalistic knowledge to the cause.

It didn't stop at one copy. We churned out thousands, even designing and writing some ourselves. However, we needed someone we could trust to distribute the leaflets, not only in Johannesburg, but across the country and overseas. Tom and Patrick travelled extensively with their jobs, so they were the obvious choice; they didn't need much persuasion to join us.

Our aim was to support others in peacefully challenging the oppressive political agenda which denied human rights to those of a different colour or race, the proviso being that we would never undertake or condone any form of violence. We'd seen enough of that in Ireland. But in the excitement of subterfuge had we really considered the possible consequences? I'm not sure.

Reality soon set in, with a vengeance. The political landscape was changing and there was a crack-down on anti-government demonstrations. Police raids were taking place all over Johannesburg; people were detained without charge, or worse simply disappeared.

We knew it was only a matter of time before we attracted the attention of BOSS, the Bureau of State Security. The four of us were questioned several times on the grounds that we were promoting anti-government propaganda. However, they had no hard evidence and each time they were forced to let us go without charge.

But we were under no illusions. Our names were known to the establishment and the possibility of arrest became real. Eventually the luck of the Irish finally ran out and we ended up on trial at the high court. Our crimes? Transmitting banned political radio programmes; circulating banned newspaper articles and leaflets, and facilitating the printing and distribution of anti-government literature.

They tried to charge me with possessing an illegal firearm and holding equipment to make explosives, but it was a trumped-up charge. Sure, they'd found a gun in my car, but it was licensed and would only be used for emergency protection. And anyway, didn't everyone in South Africa own a firearm? But explosives? Never.

The judge sentenced Patrick, Tom and Declan to ten years each and that same day they were on their way to separate prisons across the country; Durban, East London and Bloemfontein.

Then it was my turn. Louisa was allowed to bring fresh clothes for the court proceedings, but they wouldn't let her in to see me. I knew I didn't look good. I was stick-thin, pasty-faced and my new blue suit hung on me like a rag. To complete the picture, my naturally extra-large head was now topped with a long unruly mop of wiry ginger hair, which made me look completely out of proportion. Or, as one of the guards whispered on the way to the dock,

'You'll not impress the judge today Mr. O'Connell, you look like a red-headed stick-insect!' At least I'd given someone something to laugh about!

The court-room was packed with friends and colleagues. I could see Louisa on the third row, clutching Nadine's hand. My strong, brave Louisa seemed so fragile; her beautiful face looked drawn and pale; her eyes glistened with tears, and she constantly bit her bottom lip. But I was more shocked to see my daddy sitting next to her.

I hadn't seen him since I left Ireland; he looked old and tired. He'd never been out of Belfast, let alone flown in an aeroplane, and there he was, sitting ram-rod straight in his best Irish tweed, head held high, his ginger hair matching mine.

He looked directly at me. He had that stern look about him, the one he had when I was a naughty child, and then he smiled, a lop-sided rueful smile of encouragement and support. He mouthed something to me. I knew exactly what he was saying, *Prayer and patience Sean, prayer and patience*, another reminder of my childhood. Sure, but it was good to see him.

The judge turned towards me, 'Mr O'Connell, will you please stand for sentencing.' He paused for a moment, then continued. 'You have been found guilty on two counts. The first, of being an enemy of the state.'

His voice sounded grave and I had a deep sense of foreboding.

'On the second count Mr O'Connell you have been found guilty of contravening the *Explosives and Fire-arms Act*. You illegally possessed a firearm and explosive materials to make bombs, with intent to do harm. These are very serious charges and I hereby sentence you to twenty years' imprisonment.'

The court-room buzzed with shock.

I heard Louisa's sharp intake of breath, followed by a whispered, 'No Sean, no.'

'What!' I couldn't believe my ears. Where did this come from? As far as I was concerned that charge had been dropped. 'It's all bloody lies,' I yelled. 'This is not justice. Yes, I own a hand-gun, but I've a license, and the idea I'd make bombs is ridiculous.'

Anger and frustration took over and I banged my clenched fists on the bench; the handcuffs smashed on the wood and the sound of the metal chains reverberated around the room. I ranted on, 'I've been set up by the bloody police. Where's the bloody evidence?'

But the judge was not moved. 'Mr. O' Connell, this will not help your case. You have the right of appeal if you so wish. Officers take him down.' In seconds I was surrounded by guards, bundled out of the court and into a waiting prison van.

It was a long, uncomfortable drive to Cape Town and a relief to finally arrive at the prison.

But the admission process gave me a stark indication of what lay ahead. After the humiliating experience of being stripped naked and every inch of my body brutally searched, I was given a bar of carbolic soap and forced to stand under a cold shower. The guards meanwhile casually smoked a cigarette, each taking a drag and passing it round, taking great delight in watching my discomfort at the whole embarrassing episode.

Eventually one of them handed me the standard prison garb of dark blue tunic and trousers with *Prisoner* stamped on the back.

'Here, put these on,' he said, stuffing my own clothes into a paper bag. 'You won't need that suit. You think it's too big for you now? It'll be falling off your back when you get out, in twenty years. But you can have these,' throwing my trainers at me, 'at least your feet won't shrink,' he added, laughing at his own joke.

I bent down and put them on. 'Where are the laces?' I asked, 'I'll look scruffy without laces.'

This led to more laughter, 'We don't want you to hang yourself Mr. O'Connell.'

Why on earth did I ask that? Nobody would care what I looked like where I was going.

Once again I was handcuffed and placed in leg irons. The prison guards marched me outside and across a quadrangle; for a few precious minutes I felt the healing warmth of the sun, but it was short lived. We stopped outside a metal door. The guard looked at me, 'This, Mr. O'Connell,' he announced, 'is the West Wing. No-one escapes from here, except in a box.'

My whole body was taken over by convulsive shivers of fear. 'Ag shame, Mr O'Connell,' one of the other guards sneered, 'you cold? Well there's no heating in this place and we're almost in winter, it will only get worse.' I could feel my left eye swelling. I'd accidentally tripped and banged into a door, with a little help from a guard, and I was sure my ribs were broken. Breathing was still painful from a previous incident, but I knew there was no point in complaining, it would only make matters worse, and who would I complain to?

As we walked down the corridor of cells I could hear the sound of metal on metal, a deafening drumming sound, malevolent in its intensity. The guard laughed, 'Don't you worry Mr O'Connell,' he said, 'they're just practising drumming with spoons on the bars. They'll soon stop. There's been a bit of trouble, but we'll sort it out. Praat jy Afrikaans?'

'Yes. I speak a little Afrikaans.'

He nodded, 'Ja goed, that is good. Some of the officers don't speak English.' Perhaps he wasn't so bad, I thought, at least he was trying to be helpful.

We turned a corner into another long corridor; the scene was chaotic. A group of emaciated prisoners were being herded along, encouraged by guard dogs. 'These prisoners have been working in the gardens,' the guard explained, 'they make a lot of problems for us. They must learn their place and do as they are told.' I'll be sure to know my place, I thought, as I saw truncheons and revolver butts connect with flinching arms and shoulders.

From behind the bars inmates jeered and spat at the guards; I watched in horror as a body bag was dragged towards the exit. The evil intent of one particular guard was clear. 'That could be you next,' he muttered.

I knew the conditions would be poor - but this. I now understood the meaning of visceral fear.

We stopped outside an open cell, my handcuffs and leg irons removed and I was pushed inside. As I crashed to the floor I heard a terrifying scream, then realised it was mine. The guard laughed. They seemed to do a lot of laughing, but I didn't feel like joining in. 'You'll soon get used to it Mr O'Connell,' he said, 'but it's no use screaming, there's no-one to hear,' and slammed the metal door shut.

The key turned. I was alone in a prison-cell, hundreds of miles from home.

I guessed the space was about ten feet by eight, more generous than I expected, but the grey stone walls decorated with stains and graffiti were certainly depressing - and it stank! I'd never been very good with smells, not even the babies' nappies, but this was disgusting; a nauseous mixture of the stale sweat of unwashed human bodies and excrement. I forced myself to swallow a retch, the bile tasted bitter on my tongue. Perhaps I would become immune to it in time.. As expected the furnishings were sparse and utilitarian; no bed just a sisal mat, a blanket roll and in the middle a small table and chair. Behind the door stood a bucket with a lid, the tell-tale stains told me it was the lavatory.

Of course, there would be the ubiquitous bible, this being a very religious country! Sure enough, there it was on the table, keeping company with a tin plate, a mug and a spoon. Not that a bible was any use to me, I'd given up on religion long ago, much to the annoyance of Father Denny, the catholic priest who promised me a swift passage to hell unless I attended mass and confession. Maybe I'd resurrect religion if it would get me out of this place every Sunday for a couple of hours.

I was saved from total claustrophobia by a tiny skylight. It had no glass, just thick iron bars, but I could see a small patch of blue and a wisp of white cloud. I turned my face to the ceiling to catch the drift of cool sweet air. With a profound sense of sadness, I realised that precious link to the sky would be my mind's freedom in the months ahead.

Bizarrely, Solzhenitsyn's book, *One Day in the Life of Ivan Denisovich,* jumped into my head. I'd read it years ago; it portrayed one day as a prisoner in a Russian labour camp, but that was just one day of hell, a quick calculation told me I had about seven-thousand, three-hundred days to serve.

Perhaps I should start marking the days on the wall like Alexander Manette in *A Tale of Two Cities*? Or count the number of paces I did every day? I couldn't remember which book that was from.

What on earth was my mind doing? I started to laugh out loud. Why did these classic stories of prisoners keep jumping into my head? Was I delusional? Hallucinating? It was probably hysteria.

Realistically I knew there'd be no time off for good behaviour and accidental deaths were not unknown, but on the bright side at least I'd been given permission to appeal. Sure now, wasn't that just the luck of the Irish? I started to laugh again, until I found myself sobbing uncontrollably, big belly sobs I'd been holding back for weeks.

Eventually the mayhem subsided. The guards rounded up the prisoners and marched them from the corridor. The cells quietened and I lost track of time until the rusty hatch in the door grated open. 'Fetch your plate and mug,' the guard ordered. He slopped some sort of meat stew on the plate with a dollop of mealie pap and threw a chunk of dry white bread on top. It looked and smelled rancid. Then he filled the tin mug with hot sweet tea, at least I could wash the food down with that. 'It's lekker, eh?' he sniggered.

The food certainly couldn't be described as good, but I knew I had to eat it if I was to survive. I also knew that if I kept out of trouble I would be given visiting rights and allowed certain privileges; food parcels, extra clothes, books and writing materials. It was amazing, I mused, how much I knew about prison life without ever being in one.

That June night fell cold and fast. I sat at the table, pulled the thin blanket around my weary shoulders and cupped my hands round the tin mug, it was still warm from the scalding tea. Closing my eyes, I thought about Louisa and my boys.

In the silence I heard a light tapping, it was barely perceptible and seemed to come from the corner. I felt a smile creep across my face, which book was this from? Was my imagination playing tricks? But then I heard it again. Yes! I definitely heard it. What verminous creature had chosen me for a cell-mate? The phrase, *better to know thine enemies*, sprang to mind as I shuffled across the room and peered behind the rolled-up mat. There were no tell-tale signs of rats or mice, not even a cockroach. The tapping came again.

Three light taps. I grabbed the spoon from the table, and with my face to the wall knelt down as if in prayer, and tapped back. Just three taps. I had no idea who was behind that wall, but I wasn't going to miss a chance to communicate with another human being. There was a pause, then one slightly louder tap, as if to acknowledge me, then silence. But that one tap was enough. I wasn't alone.

I heard the guard shouting, 'Ligte uit. Lights out.' The lights snapped off. I lay down on the sisal mat and wrapped myself in the blanket. In the darkness I resolved that this would be my last day of self-pity. I knew what to do; keep out of trouble, start the appeals process to commute my sentence and stay alive. And with those thoughts whirling around in my head, I sank into the welcome cocoon of sleep.

The following day I discovered that the prisoner in the adjoining cell was a Joseph Martin, a retired teacher. He'd joined the ANC in its struggle against apartheid and was in for a similar crime, passing banned information. By some miraculous twist of fate, I was allocated to work with him in the library. A previous inmate had managed to set fire to the annexe where it was housed and Joe was given the task of salvaging, sorting and cataloguing as many books as possible. He saved my sanity.

Louisa made the round trip of three-thousand kilometres every month and for thirty short minutes she kept me up-to-date with the world outside. We laughed at the antics of the twins, now walking and chattering and generally up to mischief. We discussed the appeal, which was going well, and Louisa even managed to sweet-talk the guards into allowing me extra writing materials in exchange for home-made cakes and cigarettes. Of course, she was an Afrikaaner - one of them!

Over the next few months I managed to keep my head down and stay out of trouble. Every day was the same; work, eat, sleep, plus an hour's exercise in the quadrangle. I read anything I could get my hands on; made a papier-maché chess set from discarded pages of fire-damaged books and played through the cell wall with Joe. I helped Stefan, the Afrikaans night warder, improve his spoken English in return for a weekly newspaper and wrote and illustrated stories about Irish folklore for my two boys. Anything to keep my mind active. And then one morning, at two o'clock, they came for me.

I woke to find a torch shining in my face. 'Come Sean, get dressed.' It was Stefan. He handed me a rucksack. I recognised it as the one I came in with. 'Here are your things; pack anything else you wish to keep.' I opened my mouth to speak, but he stopped me, 'There is no time, do not ask questions.' Then his voice softened, 'I'll tell Joe.' Now I was scared.

Stefan was joined by another warder and I was marched out of the cell, down the corridor, across the quadrangle and through a side gate to a waiting black car. 'We'll leave you here,' Stefan said and held out his hand to shake mine, 'Totsiens, goodbye and go well Mr O'Connell.'

Why no handcuffs or leg irons? It didn't make sense. Two men in dark suits sat either side of me in the back seat. I asked where we were going, 'Jo'burg,' one of them replied.

We drove through the night. Conversation was minimal. Perhaps I was being transferred to the Old Fort Prison? At least I would be closer to Louisa. Eventually I stopped trying to talk and fell asleep.

Dawn broke and the driver pulled up at a roadside stall for coffee and breakfast. Should I make a run for it? But when I caught sight of the tell-tale bulky shape of guns under their jackets I decided it wouldn't be a wise move.

By mid-day the sun was high in a clear blue sky and as we approached Johannesburg I began to recognise its famous landmarks. To the right the huge toxic mine dumps, left by the gold rush in 1886, dominated the sky-line. Directly ahead the Hertzog Communications Tower seemed to command the city and to my left I could see the airport traffic-control tower. Then I knew.

We skirted around the perimeter fence of Jan Smuts airport and stopped near a side entrance. I was handed over to two waiting policemen and marched down endless grey corridors, in silence, to a small room. A uniformed official sat behind a table, 'Meneer O'Connell,' he said. 'I am Major Theron and I am here to inform you that today you will be deported to England. You have no right to appeal this decision and will not be allowed to re-enter South Africa.'

He gestured to the man standing next to him, 'My colleague, Captain Lawrie, will escort you on the next flight to London. At Heathrow he will stay with you until officials from the British foreign office and immigration arrive to escort you from the aircraft. You will then be under their jurisdiction.'

That old cliché, *my heart sank,* was so true! I felt it plummet into my belly. I swallowed hard, then asked the question, dreading the answer, 'What about my wife and children?'

'They have elected to travel with you and will join you on board the aircraft.' He handed me a brown envelope, 'Here is your passport and wallet. You will find everything is in order. Good luck.' Ten minutes later, escorted by Captain Lawrie, I climbed the steps and boarded the huge aircraft.

'Why?' I asked Louisa, once we got over the delighted shock of our reunion.

'I don't know. I was visited by the Bureau of State Security who explained that you would be deported, but as I am a South African national and the children have dual nationality, I could choose to stay. They warned me that if I go with you there is no guarantee I will be allowed re-entry in the future. The others, Declan, Patrick and Tom, have already gone; their families are due to fly out next week. I don't know why we are being allowed to travel together... but who cares?'

At exactly 18.45pm, the Boeing 707, flight number BA018 left Jan Smuts airport, its destination London Heathrow and freedom.

Epilogue

After a meeting with British officials at Heathrow Airport, Sean and his family were allowed to travel on to Belfast. There was a rumour that the British foreign office had done a deal with the South African government. But the real story behind the release of the four Irish journalists was never revealed. It was made clear that for the foreseeable future they would be refused entry to South Africa.

TB The Killer

I am the Killer.
I want to be known to all nations,
both rich and poor.
I don't discriminate.

I love your chest where I live.
You can never be clever
when it comes to me and my sister HIV.
We enjoy being together in your body.

When I come to you
I come like a quiet enemy,
to destroy you.
If you are not careful
you will not even suspect I am there.
So be warned

Zolani Ganya Age 14.
Kwanokolo

The N2 North to Cape Town

I understood why Zolani was stir crazy. Twenty-two years of age and we still lived with Ma, Pa and toothless Ouma, in a two-roomed shack in Gugulethu Township. We were about three weeks old and barely alive when a ranger found us abandoned in the bush. Elvira and Ebraim took us in, just until our mother came to fetch us, but she never came. And so we stayed.

We called them Ma and Pa and they christened me Simphiwe and my twin brother Zolani. "Ja," Ma would laugh, "you were both so skinny even the hyena would not eat you, so we fattened you up in case the lion came to call."

She was the best Ma, full of hugs, but so strict. We must go to school and church, keep clean and tidy and when she put the tin tub outside in the sunshine and the pans of water on the fire to boil there was no argument - it was bath day!

Even the neighbours knew, they would point and laugh as we were stripped naked then scrubbed and rubbed until our black skins were nearly red and our hair washed and combed until it was nearly straight. But then she would smooth our skin with oil from the glycerine palm until we were burnished ebony, wrap us in blankets and sit us on her fat dimply knees,

"Do you know how the olifant got his trunk?" she would whisper, then weave a web of magical bush-tales while we licked the sticky syrup-dripping koeksisters she'd deep fried that day.

We didn't look like twins or think like twins. Zolani was big, strong and streetwise; always part of a gang. I think he was born angry; his wide black nostrils would flare until they almost covered his face and he roared like a mad bull until he got his way. But he did not scare me and I did not blame him for being angry. He didn't want to live in a shack in a township, he just wanted a nice house and a television. What was wrong with that?

And me? I was small and skinny and dreamed of being a poet, or a ranger in a game reserve. I was sooo lucky when the school helped me get voluntary work with a local travel company. My job was to go with the ranger taking tourists on safari to spot the 'Big Five'. I didn't get any pay, just food and a uniform, but I was trained by Komani, an ancient bush-tracker; his bandy legs could track spoor for miles and he knew every creature and plant.

"What do you see Simphiwe?" he would ask, and the huge grey body of a rhino with her calf would lumber through the thorn thicket, or a mangy lion dragging a squealing springbok. But best of all the rangers taught me to drive so I could get my licence and drive the safari bus.

After a year I was given a khaki shirt with 'Zebra Tours' on the pocket and a green shiny badge which said, 'Simphiwe. Assistant Ranger'. At last I was on a pay-roll.

Ma was proud, 'Do you think they have a job for your brother?' she asked. But Zolani was not interested in the bush; he didn't care about learning, didn't even finish school and was always in trouble. Ma begged, threatened and bribed him to go back to school; she did everything she could to make him see sense, but he seethed at the injustice of his life.

We argued, as brothers do, but gradually his tone changed from banter to anger and one morning he exploded.

'I hate this place Simphi,' he said. 'I've walked for twenty minutes to the standpipe for water, but it was dry.' He flung the plastic water carrier across the floor, 'Hell bro, I'm not living like this any longer. It's 2015, twenty-four years since apartheid finished, but nothing's changed. Ja, we're allowed to live in the 'white areas' and go to 'white schools', but how can we afford it? And anyway, you never see white children in the township schools.

'What happened to Mandela's promises man? When will there be jobs and roads? Look around you man; Ma's sick, she needs a proper house with clean water from a proper tap.'

I knew better than agree or disagree with him, it just made things worse, anyway I knew he was right. But what could I do?

'It is as it is Zoli,' I said, as he stomped off, 'things will get better, we must be patient.' I knew he would never be that and I worried about what he might do.

Ma was very thin and tired; she coughed all night, sometimes all day. She said it was worry, but the Doctor said it was the TB. Every week she must go to the clinic for medicines and a food parcel, then she would get better, but the medicines made her sick, so she didn't take them. And she couldn't go to the clinic every week, the bus didn't go there, and we didn't always have money for the taxi. She seemed to have given up and was often on her knees weeping and praying.

And Pa? He would sit outside in front of the brazier with his friends and drink beer and smoke betel leaves, which made his mind fly away somewhere else. Sometimes they would all fall asleep and scorch their legs, and Ma would scold them, then treat the burns with ointment she'd made from the aloe-vera plant.

But they never learned! They would still sit and chit-chat until the fire went cold.

"Ag man, those days in the homelands were the best," Pa would reminisce. And the old fools would nod their drunken heads, "Ja ja Ebraim, that is true."

I worried about Zolani. Twice he'd been locked up in the Youth Centre, where the kids mixed with adult prisoners, took drugs and became better criminals. Now *he* was a grown-up and mixed with the tsotsis who carried guns and machetes, smoked dagga and spread HIV/ Aids.

Zolani said he never did any of those things, but I didn't believe him. I also knew he had two babas with different girls. 'Neer man, not me,' he said. His eyes crinkled and his fleshy lips curled into a wide grin, 'there are no baba Zolanis in Gugulethu.'

It was past midnight when I heard him. 'Zoli, where you going man?' I asked.

'None of your business Simphi.'

'They'll catch you and send you to a proper prison, then you'll never get out.' I warned.

'Look!' He grabbed my head and forced my face down to the stinking bucket in the corner, 'Why can't we have a proper toilet? And there's Ouma on a plastic mattress on the floor, grunting and snoring like a warthog, she needs a proper bed.'

He ranted on, swearing and cursing, 'Ten bladdy years since Mandela promised us houses, where are the bladdy houses? You tell me. Some of us will change that, you'll see.'

'I hear you bro.' I didn't know what else to say.

'And don't follow,' he hissed. The corrugated tin walls reverberated like a thunder sheet as he slammed the door and disappeared into the maze of shacks.

I heard Ma call, 'What is it Simphiwe?'

'Nothing Ma. Go to sleep.'

I knew I would have to follow him.

Streaks of smoke from dampened braziers drifted low in ghostly tendrils across the sleeping township, but there was enough moon to see, so ignoring the half-hearted yaps of the yard dogs and startled moans of tethered cows, I chased after him. I knew every twist and turn of this township, especially how to avoid the gullies when the giant rubber sewage buckets hadn't been emptied and they overflowed onto the dirt tracks, and the stench floated up your nose and in your mouth.

I soon caught up with Zoli. He'd stopped near the church where a huge billboard showed a picture of a young black couple. Holding hands and smiling they pointed to its message, *Be Smart. Abstain and Live.* Was this the Church's answer to contraception? I stifled a laugh. Someone had added a speech bubble and scribbled, *'If you don't give us condoms we'll get HIV'*, and pinned a bunch of rubbers to his outstretched hand. What would Father Patrick make of that?

Almost immediately a clapped-out bakkie pulled up. Zolani greeted the driver, 'Andre, you ok?'

'Ja man,' he replied. Another figure jumped from the passenger side. I recognised Voyu, he was big trouble. They squatted by the roadside, heads together, whispering. I inched closer, straining to hear, then I caught the sweet sickly smell of dagga as they passed a joint round. After a few minutes Zoli stood up; I heard the trickle of water as he peed against the wheel, before climbing into the driver's seat. He didn't have a driving licence, but then I didn't know many in the townships who did.

The three men continued talking quietly. 'Ok. We'll go Settlers and N2,' I heard Zoli say. I crept round the back of the truck and as the engine spluttered into life I pulled myself over the tail-gate and dropped quietly onto a pile of car tyres. I was surrounded by petrol cans and sacks of rocks, partly covered with a tarpaulin, so I crouched behind the cab and pulled the filthy oilskin over me.

The truck lurched and rattled down the pot-holed tracks. Eventually the surface evened out and I knew we were on Settlers Way and would soon hit the N2 motorway going north into Cape Town. We stopped at the top of the slip-road and pulled onto the hard shoulder. I could hear the men shouting and laughing as they unloaded the bakkie. Zolani was clearly in charge, 'Voyu, catch, pass to Andre,' he ordered, as he threw the tyres off the truck.

They were too high on dagga and beer to notice me, so I peered over the side and watched them pile the tyres in the middle lane, then slosh the petrol over.

A match flared. The slicks of oily petrol ignited. Five, ten seconds and, whoosh.

The fire travelled fast across the lanes, engulfing the funeral pyres of rubber; blue and orange flames leaped and streaked into the night, sending the dead tyres on their last journey. The crazy men whooped and cheered as they danced round the bonfires, and as black acrid smoke smothered the highway they scattered sacks of rocks onto the hard shoulder, ready for the street kids to hurl at the early morning traffic. The intention was to cause maximum disruption and bring terror to the unsuspecting commuters.

I now knew where my brother had been when he disappeared at night and came back smelling of petrol and smoke.

I was sure the police and fire service would soon be on the scene and hoped Zolani had the sense to head back to the township; there would be no mercy if they were caught. But no, the bakkie careered down the motorway and screeched to a halt at the next exit. I wriggled under the tarpaulin, pressed my body against the floor and prayed.

Zoli switched off the engine and jumped from the cab,

'Voyu,' he called, 'there are only a few tyres left, you take over the driving. Be ready to move when I say.' As he dropped the tail-gate he caught sight of me, 'Hell man! You bladdy dummkopf,' he whispered, 'keep quiet,' and kicked the remaining tyres onto the highway. 'Andre,' he shouted, 'pile these on the fast lane.' He glared at me and put his fingers to his lips, then banged on the side of the cab, 'Okay Voyu, it's getting light, let's get out of here, fast.'

I wasn't expecting his next move. In one powerful action he grabbed me under the armpits, hauled me up and dropped me onto the roadside, 'Voetzek, run, go home.' He wasn't going to kill me – yet!

I flew across the scrubland and dived behind a huge aloe to catch my breath. Their over-excited voices carried in the still night. The flames flickered and crackled, then blazed through the haze, and the silhouette of Table Mountain emerged through the lightening sky.

Without warning flood-lights swept the highway. A tannoy boomed from the shadows,

'Police. Stop. Stay where you are. Put your hands in the air.'

'Run bro,' I heard Zoli shout. Gun shots followed me as I streaked across the wasteland and I didn't stop until I reached the safety of the gloomy labyrinth that was Gugulethu.

I waited up, but Zoli didn't come back that night and by morning talk of the shooting was all over the township. I listened to the news on the radio.

Two policemen shot dead and another injured on the N2 north to Cape Town. Five-thousand rands reward for any information.

Every day the township swarmed with police armed with guns and sjamboks. Road blocks stopped all traffic going in and out of Gugulethu; drivers and passengers questioned. Helicopters constantly clattered and whirred low over the shacks, well into the night; dog handlers patrolled every corner, struggling to control the straining snarling Alsatians and Rhodesian Ridgebacks.

Ma was worried, 'Do you think Zolani was involved? Where is he?' she asked.

Pa suspected I knew something, 'Simphiwe, you must tell me if he is in trouble.' But I dare not say, so I went to work as usual and tried to act normally.

Then the third policeman died and the search intensified. They found the burned-out bakkie; it had no plates and no one reported it missing.

The township was jumpy. The tsotsis vanished from street corners; yard dogs whined, unsettled in the tense atmosphere and Mammas kept the kids inside. The police raided the shacks, dragging men away in armoured vans for interrogation. Zolani was well known to them, so they came to our place several times; asking questions, searching. But Ma had hidden his stuff, and Pa, who would never tell a lie, told them he'd gone to Johannesburg to find work. Eventually they were convinced we knew nothing, and anyway they were frightened they would catch TB from Ma, so we made her cough as much as possible.

Three months later we received a message to say that Zoli was in Durban.

It was two years before I saw him again.

I smelled the dagga before he crept into the bedroom. He was the real spiv in his sharp suit and gold watch, flashy rings on each hand: he looked thin and drawn, but had lost none of his swagger.

'Ja Simphiwe, life's bladdy good,' he said. 'I got a VW Kombi, a proper house and a good woman in Durban. You must come visit, perhaps get a job as a ranger in Hluhuwe game reserve. Ja man, that would be good.'

I told him we'd been allocated a brick house with electricity, a toilet and running water; it would have 2 bedrooms, a living room, kitchen, bathroom and a yard where I could grow vegetables. We would move in four weeks.

Zolani was full of excited promises, 'I'll get a good doctor for Ma, a rocking-chair for Pa, a proper bed for Ouma and a television for you.' He paused and looked at me, 'Perhaps once the bladdy polisie have stopped looking for me I can come visit some more?'

I had to tell him. 'Zolani, Ma passed over in June last year and after she'd gone Ouma just faded away. They're buried next to each other in Gugulethu graveyard. There's only Pa and me.'

He flopped down on the bed and looked at me as if he didn't understand what I was saying. His voice sounded puzzled, almost childlike, 'How could she die without seeing me? Why didn't she wait for me?' Then I felt his anger. His voice got louder, until he was shouting. 'Hell bro, why didn't she wait? She knew I'd come, I sent a message and told her I'd be back. Why didn't you let me know Simphi?'

'How could I? I never had your address. And how could she wait Zoli? You knew how ill she was.'

Without warning he smashed his fist on the goat-skin drum Pa made when we were little; the sound bounced off the tin walls and echoed, over and over again, which set the yard dogs barking. His face twisted with rage, he was that angry little boy again, but this time I was scared.

He jumped up and stood over me, 'Look at me Simphi,' he yelled, pointing to his suit, 'see this? Look at my smart clothes, and look at this,' he said, flashing his watch, 'it's solid gold. I wanted to tell Ma about my house and new life; I wanted her be proud of me, just like she was of you.'

He prowled up and down the room, up and down. 'I've gone legit bro; I got a business selling things, from a proper shop. I don't do those bad things anymore. In a couple of years I was going to send for you all to come and live with me in Durban, away from this stinking hole. I just wanted her to see me do good and now I've got the bladdy AIDS. Yes Simphi, AIDs and if the medicines don't work I'll be joining her. What bladdy good's that? Eh? Eh Simphiwe? You tell me.'

I caught a fleeting glance of fear in his eyes, and for a few moments there was silence. I wasn't shocked he had AIDs, nearly everyone I knew had it, but I wasn't sure what to say. I just knew I had to try to calm his thoughts.

'Ag shame you got the AIDs Zolani,' I said, 'but the treatment's good, you'll be right.'

I paused, 'and anyway, Ma knew you would turn out okay, she said so.'

He whipped round, and before I knew it he had gripped me by the throat, lifted me off the floor and eyeballed me.

'What do you know about it?' His huge lips curled in a sneer, 'You, the clever one, the animal lover, the God lover, always doing the right…' He stopped and stared past me. His eyes widened in his pinched face, 'Pa?' he whispered and loosened his grip on me.

Gasping for air I followed his gaze. Pa stood by the curtain that separated our bed space; he looked ancient in his woolly hat, a faded blanket wrapped round his shoulders and his long undies tucked into odd socks to keep the goggas from biting his legs.

'Zolani,' he said, his voice soft and gentle, 'come, sit by me,' and stretched out his hand.

I could hear murmurs from behind the curtain, I don't know what Pa said, but it went quiet. Then I heard it. A low trumpet-rumble sound of distress, like that of an elephant mourning her dead calf. It came from deep inside Zoli's belly, followed by an anguished howl. I rushed outside, my hands over my ears to block out his pain, and I wept for my brother.

The sun was almost up and the last piece of wood smouldering on the brazier when Zoli came to sit by me; his face puffy, his eyes swollen and red-rimmed. There was so much to be said, and there was nothing to be said.

I spoke first. 'I never knew you felt like that about me; that you thought I was the clever one and that Ma loved me the most. She didn't. She loved us both the same.'

'I know,' he said, his voice low and sad.

'What will you do?'

'I'll go to Durban to get the treatment. And you Simphi? Are you still a ranger?'

'Ja, I'm qualified now, but the church has offered to sponsor me to study to be a pastor.'

He nodded and smiled, 'You'll be a lekker pastor.'

In the morning he was quiet as he said goodbye to Pa, and when he put his arm round my shoulders it felt like the weight of the world. He pressed a thick wad of notes into my hand, 'Totsiens little bro, look after Pa.'

I never asked who fired the shots and I never saw him again.

Mountain Treachery

*The narrow path, bestrewn with flowers,
grew steeper as the sun rose higher.
Upon the top, the white cloth clouds
swirl and drift in graceful lines,
and from the clouds the curlews swoop
and peck discarded crumbs
the hikers threw in careless thought.*

*At last the summit, grassy flat,
gave welcome to those weary legs.
They leaned upon the wooden rail
and gasped in awe this cliff top view
of glittering seas and silver sands,
of white foam waves and treacherous reefs
enticing them to plunge beneath.*

*The wind whipped round, the sky turned grey,
no sun to sparkle on this table top.
Storm clouds rolled in. Vision blurring
unseen dangers in this changing scene.
No signal here. No calls from home
for stranded souls, their fate unknown.*

Ultimate Betrayal

Marisa stared at the grim brick building with its impenetrable walls topped with rolls of rusting barbed wire.

It had taken almost six hours to drive from Bloemfontein to Pretoria and now she wondered what she was doing there.

Exhausted, she rested her head on the steering wheel and thought about what the man on the phone had said.

"There are seven spaces for hangings at Pretoria's Central Prison, Miss, but on that day, there'll only be five. The prisoners will stand in a line; each one will have a rope placed around their neck and a white hood over their head, then the executioner will pull a lever."

One of the five was Petrus Sebezela.

The guard checked her permit, and the heavy gates swung open. She followed the signs to the visitor's entrance; the car park was empty, so she parked in a bay close to the door. She looked at her watch - it was six o'clock. She'd driven through the night and was early, but the man hadn't been able to give an accurate time of the proceedings.

"Probably about eight o'clock," he'd said, "but you can wait."

Grabbing her bag and a small bunch of flowers from the passenger seat, she slid out of the yellow sports car, walked the few yards to the entrance and pressed the intercom button.

'Naam?' a voice demanded.

'Marisa du Toit,' she replied.

The door swung open. A heavy-set man in a dark blue uniform and peaked cap stood behind a desk. He looked up. His eyes widened. He wasn't used to seeing young women in this part of the prison, especially white women like this one. Tall and willowy in a smart navy trouser suit, her dark hair cropped short, she was stunning and oozed confidence and wealth.

He swallowed hard, 'Your permit please, Miss du Toit.'

She fished in her bag, produced a brown envelope and offered it to him. He removed the document and scrutinised it. 'I.D. card please.'

Without a word Marisa handed it over.

The officer looked ready for retirement. His crumpled face, almost hidden by a bushy white moustache, expressed concern. 'Are you sure you want to be here Miss?' he asked. 'It's not a place for young ladies.

'Quite sure.'

He shrugged, 'Okay. Down the corridor, first door on the left - you can wait there. We'll let you know when it's over.'

He watched as she walked down the corridor, high heels tapping on the concrete floor, and wondered why she was interested in Sebezeli; he was just another murdering Black.

Marisa looked around the visitors' room; small but clean there was just enough space for a table and two wooden chairs. The morning sun failed to pierce the dirty barred window and the room seemed to exude sadness and despair. Or was that a reflection of her own feelings? With a deep sigh she placed the pale cream roses on the table. She didn't know why she'd brought them; everyone took flowers to funerals... but executions? Removing her jacket, she draped it over the back of a chair and sat down, straight backed and still, and waited.

Ten minutes later the door opened and a priest appeared, balancing two mugs of tea on a tin tray. He smiled and held out his free hand, 'Good morning, Miss du Toit, or may I call you Marisa?'

'Yes,' her voice quiet and weary.

'I'm Father Joseph Loubart, one of the prison chaplains. The duty officer was worried about you so he's made you some of his special Rooibos tea. Do you mind if I sit with you for a while?' adding, almost apologetically, 'I'm afraid I'm the only one available.'

Marisa shook her head, she didn't care who sat with her.

'I know you've come to say goodbye to Petrus Sebelezi,' he continued, taking a sip of the steaming tea. 'I met Petrus a few times in prison. He seemed a nice boy, just someone who'd lost his way.'

She nodded, 'He wasn't always a bad person.'

For a while they sat in silence, then Marisa asked, 'Do you know if he talked about me?'

'Not to me, but he did ask for forgiveness for his crime. I spoke to him last night and he was genuinely sorry for what he had done.' Another silence.

The priest tried again, 'Had you known Petrus long?'

'I have always known him.'

He leaned towards her, inviting her to confide in him, 'Sometimes it helps to talk, or we could say a prayer for him.'

She met his gaze, her ashen face impassive. He didn't look like a priest, he was tall and thin with greying hair that curled tight to his head; he wore his robes with elegance. There was a calmness about him. His dark eyes focussed on her, steady and reassuring. She sensed an inner strength and instinctively trusted him.

'I don't believe in God,' she said. 'I did once, but not now.'

He smiled, 'Then I will pray for you and Petrus.'

Marisa placed the half-empty mug on the table and walked over to the window.

'You want to know about Petrus?' The priest nodded. 'It's a long story,' she said, fiddling with the strap on her bag.

'We have time,' he reassured her, 'and they say I'm a good listener.'

She appeared lost in thought for a moment, a wistful expression on her face, then began to tell her story.

'Petrus lived on our farm in the Free State with Nomsa his adoptive mother, who was my nanny … fat as butter Nomsa with no front teeth. Nomsa, who did the housework with me wrapped in a kanga and slung on her back, and Petrus, who was three years old, clinging onto her overalls. Or so he told me. I still remember her crooning to me, "Thula baba, Hush baba," until I was asleep.

'I loved Nomsa. She was the first person I saw in the morning and the last one at night.' Marisa smiled to herself, 'For a while I thought she was my mother, but the Pastor soon put me straight. "Marisa," he said, "Nomsa can't be your mother, your mother must be white like you. Nomsa is black, she's just a servant."

'So I knew from an early age that I was born on the right side of apartheid; white, wealthy and privileged,' an edge of bitterness crept into her voice, 'while my gentle Nomsa was black, poor, and slaved for my family for a pittance. But it was she who took Petrus in after his mother died and looked after him as if he were her own.'

Marisa paused for a moment, 'I think I was a big disappointment to my mother,' she mused. 'She was so beautiful and stylish, while I was clumsy and untidy. I much preferred jeans, or shorts and T-shirts, to pretty dresses and ribbons, and I hated the afternoon tea parties she was famous for. But Pa understood, he just laughed when she complained that I never wanted to do things with her.

"She's just a tomboy," he would say, "she'll grow out of it." And so I ran wild with Petrus, while my mother turned her attention to the farm kids. She made sure they went to school, fed and wormed them and beat them when they were naughty.'

Father Joseph chuckled, 'I know just what you mean, I was brought up on a farm.'

'But you're ... coloured ... and a priest.' Marisa blurted out, astonished by this revelation. He seemed far too sophisticated to have ever been a farm-boy.

'Yes. I was born in KwaZulu-Natal. I never knew who my father was, but he was white,' adding with a wry smile, 'you know how complicated this country is. My mother worked for a strict Irish Catholic family; they had no children and so decided I should be educated and follow the Lord's pathway.

'I was lucky, I could have ended up in trouble, but they sent me to a strict Catholic boarding school. Later I went to Ireland where I studied for the priesthood. I could have stayed there, but Africa was always where I wanted to be and I needed to help support my mother. Now, tell me more about this Petrus.'

'I was also dispatched to boarding school.' Marisa explained. 'I hated it. I missed the freedom of the farm and Petrus and couldn't wait for the holidays. Sometimes my cousin Joana came over from Holland to stay - she was like a sister to me. We would spend the days roaming the homestead from morning to dusk, looking for adventures; Petrus was never far behind, he would do anything we asked.'

Marisa laughed at the memory. 'When Joana and I raced around on our ponies chasing the stupid guinea fowl he would run alongside, barefoot, determined to catch one for Nomsa to put in the pot, which he usually did. Sometimes we camped in the bush and Petrus would make a fire and sleep outside the tent to keep us safe. We were all such great friends then.

'Of course, Ma didn't approve of me spending so much time with him. "You must stay with your own kind Marisa, people will talk," she said. But I didn't care and anyway Pa trusted him.

'He used to say that *Petrus knew his place* and would make sure I was safe.

'Knew his place!' She spat out the words, 'We all know what that means… Whites are superior to Blacks and should never be allowed to mix.'

The Priest nodded, 'I know,' his voice soft and gentle, 'so many lives have been ruined by apartheid. But it will end and you will find a way forward.' He stood up, 'I'll see if I can find out what's happening.'

Marisa looked at her watch, it was already 7.30am. She felt anxious, her pulse was racing and she felt her heart pounding. Perhaps she should leave. There was nothing she could do now for Petrus, in fact she didn't really know why she was there. But as she gathered her things together to go the door opened and Father Joseph held out a mug. 'Here you are, more tea,' he said. 'I'm not sure what has happened, but it will be at least another hour before the proceedings begin.'

They sat quietly for a while, drinking the hot aromatic tea, then Marisa spoke.

'I was eighteen when I left boarding school. I was so naïve. Most of my friends had steady boyfriends, but I wasn't interested in boys. Ma did her best at match-making; she arranged dates with suitable farmers' sons and insisted I was seen in the right places. I went along with her plans; joined the Vaal yacht club and learned to sail, played tennis and partied until the early hours. But secretly I was meeting Petrus.' She looked at the priest, 'I loved him... are you shocked?'

He shook his head, 'No, just saddened at what you must have gone through.'

'We knew it was an impossible situation, but we could wait and in the meantime, make plans. It was only two years to my 21st birthday when I would inherit a considerable amount of money. Our plan was to travel to Holland where I had relatives and no-one cared about the colour of your skin.

'I hadn't seen Joana for a couple of years, then out of the blue she asked if she could spend the summer with me, before going to university. I couldn't wait to see her. But it wasn't the Joana I knew who stepped out of the car! I scarcely recognised her with her cropped blonde hair and huge white-framed sunglasses that covered her face. And her legs! Encased in white knee-high boots they seemed to go on forever and she wore the shortest of mini-skirts. She looked fantastic and just oozed confidence.

'I wasn't the only one shocked. I saw Petrus watching her from across the yard, his mouth wide open, his eyes almost popping out of his head. But despite her worldly appearance we were still best friends; the same crazy girl with a giggly outlook on life, *and* she liked my grown-up Petrus. She'd known him for years, but now he was six feet tall and *very* good looking.'

She paused, 'Do you really want to hear all this?' she asked.

'Yes, I do. Sometimes it helps to talk through things with a stranger.'

Marisa nodded. 'It soon became clear that Joana had led a much more exciting life than me. She loved to shock me with stories about her liberal life in Holland; the red-light district, night clubs, the Beatles and Twiggy.

"This is the swinging sixties Marisa," she would say, "Bloemfontein is so behind the times."

'She was determined to drag me into the modern world and in less than a week she'd convinced Pa that I should have my own clothing allowance *and* a car. Sure enough a little yellow sports car was delivered and the shopping sprees to Johannesburg began. I swapped shorts and T-shirts for mini-skirts; cropped my hair, lined my eyes with black kohl pencil and poured my newly found curves into a bikini. Petrus couldn't believe the change in me. "You are so beautiful Marisa," he said. "Perhaps you are too good for me now. Perhaps you will find a rich white boy to marry." *I knew I wouldn't.*

'Joana was so excited about our plans, but we soon realised that leaving South Africa would not be straightforward. The problem was obtaining a passport for Petrus. But the ever-positive Joana wouldn't let anything get in her way, she even offered to take Petrus to Pretoria to collect the appropriate papers and help him fill them in. I couldn't go because Ma was away and I had to help around the farm.

'I have to say I was a little bit jealous when they drove off in my car, then spent hours together completing the forms. But I knew she was doing it to help me and Petrus.'

Marisa stopped and glanced at her watch,

Do you think they've done it yet?' she asked, her voice anxious, almost fearful, 'The execution I mean.'

'No, not yet. You will hear a loud bell signalling that it is over, then you will be taken to a room where the Registrar will make the official announcement.'

Taking a relieved breath, she carried on. 'It was the last Sunday of Joana's visit. We were ready to go to church when she developed one of her famous headaches! She said she felt so dreadful she couldn't possibly go. I knew it was just an excuse to stay in bed, but Ma was away and she only had to flutter her eyes and smile at Pa to get her own way. Of course, I still had to go.

'Immediately after the service I dashed home. Joana's bedroom door was closed, I assumed she was still in bed so I hurriedly got changed, grabbed a towel and walked over to the barn to find Petrus. We'd arranged to go swimming in the river.

'Oh! I found him all right. As I crossed the yard I could hear music blaring, it was the Beatles, *'Love me Do'*, my favourite. I was singing it as I danced up the steps and pushed open the door. I could scarcely believe what was in front of me. It was Petrus and Joana, they were...' she stopped and looked at Father Joseph. A soft flush suffused her face until her cheeks were scarlet with embarrassment. 'They were *together*,' she blurted out. 'You know, *doing that...together!*'

The priest nodded his understanding, his grey eyes full of compassion 'Yes, I think I know what you mean.'

'And! They were playing *my* transistor radio.

'Joana caught sight of me first. I could see the horror in her eyes as she struggled to reach her clothes. Then Petrus looked over his shoulder, straight at me then scrabbled on the floor for his trousers and fled, Joana in hot pursuit. I just stood and wept.' Marisa blinked back the tears and closed her eyes, then walked over to the chair and sat down.

'I never slept with him,' she whispered, 'we decided we would wait until we were married.'

'That must have been a difficult moment for you,' the priest said. 'You must have felt very let down and disappointed.'

'Let down? I felt angry! More than angry. I wanted to kill him *and* Joana.' Her face contorted with grief, 'How could he betray me like that? Naturally I told Pa what they'd been up to. Joana said Petrus made her do it, but Pa didn't believe her and neither did I. The incident should have been reported to the police, but Pa decided he didn't want a scandal and would deal with the matter himself. In the end Petrus was flogged and banned from the farm.

'Joana did try to say she was sorry, "It was only sex Marisa," she said, "it didn't mean anything, I swear." But I wouldn't listen. I hated her and blamed her for throwing herself at him. I made sure she was sent home in disgrace.

'I missed Petrus so much. I couldn't eat or sleep and stopped meeting my friends. Ma and Pa were worried, but I couldn't tell them that I loved him and that's why I was so upset. I had no-one to confide in. I did try to tell Nomsa, who by then was an old lady, but she didn't want to know. She said I should forget all about him or we'd both end up in trouble with the law.'

Marisa looked at the priest, 'But you know Father, I was still convinced that once everyone had calmed down he would come back for me. I would have forgiven him and we would have been able to continue with our plans. Maybe not to Amsterdam,' she mused, 'perhaps England – but he didn't come.

'Eventually I decided I needed something to take my mind off things, away from the farm. Pa knew one of the directors of a diamond company, so I spent some time there learning the trade. Twelve months later I opened my own jewellery shop in Bloemfontein.' She looked up at the priest, 'It's doing quite well. I now have four staff and a very talented designer.'

'Did you ever see Petrus again?'

Marisa nodded, 'About three years later.'

'Oh?'

'I'd heard that he was back in the area looking for a job, but thanks to Ma none of the farmers in the area would employ him. Then Erasmus, one of the farm workers, told me Petrus was living in Manguang Township and was involved with a gang of tsotsis.

'Apparently the police pulled him over for a traffic offence, searched the vehicle and found a packet of 'pot' in the glove compartment. He was arrested for possession of drugs, fined and jailed for a week. I found it difficult to believe, it just didn't sound like the Petrus I knew. But perhaps I didn't really know him at all.

'Then Ma admitted she'd seen him several times in town driving a white bakkie and had noticed the same truck parked a couple of times on the track leading to the farm. She said it was definitely him. Sometimes he seemed to be just watching the house, other times he sat on the paddock gate feeding the horses. He loved those horses and always had his pockets full of carrots or apples for them. But he wasn't doing any harm and she hadn't mentioned it before because she didn't want to upset me. That was difficult to believe! Concern wasn't her style; it's more likely she didn't want us to become friends again.

'Erasmus told me that Petrus was hoping to see me, to ask if Ma would give him a second chance and a job on the farm. I knew she wouldn't, but I decided to keep a look out for him, perhaps we could clear the air. If we couldn't be friends at least we could be civil to one another.

'It was one Sunday afternoon when I finally saw him. I'd just returned from the tennis club and was about to go into the house when I caught sight of a white bakkie parked on the track near the paddock gate. It had to be him, so I decided to walk over and speak to him. I was about fifty yards away when the cab door opened and he climbed out. He'd filled out and his hair was very short, but he was still the same Petrus. I wasn't sure how I would feel; I think my heart stopped for a second. He stood looking towards the house then leaned over the back of the truck and lifted something out. I couldn't see what it was. Then he lit a cigarette, leapt over the gate and skirting the paddock, walked towards the yard.

'He…' Marisa suddenly stopped and stood up, she looked pale and anxious. 'I wonder if I could have a glass of water?' she asked, her voice trembling. 'It's so warm in here.'

The priest sensed she was about to tell him something significant. 'Of course,' he said. 'I think I need a cold drink too.'

Marisa walked towards the sash window to see if it would open, but it was firmly nailed down. She closed her eyes and swayed ever so slightly, then took three or four deep breaths, trying to compose her thoughts. A few minutes later the priest returned juggling a jug of iced water and two beakers. 'Sorry about the plastic,' he said, 'they don't allow glass in the prison.'

The ice cubes clinked as she gulped the cool water. 'Thank you.'

'Are you sure you want to carry on?'

She nodded, 'Quite sure. Where was I? Oh yes, Petrus was walking towards the barn. I saw him look around then open the door, just a little, then sneak inside. I'm not sure how long he was in there, just a few minutes. When he came out, he was carrying two petrol cans.

'I watched him close the door, slide the wooden bolt across and head towards the track.

'I started to run across the field and shouted to him, "Hey Petrus, wait. Hoe gaan dit met jou? How're you doing?"

'He turned and looked directly at me. He seemed to hesitate. I thought he was going to stop, but he didn't, he turned and ran towards the bakkie, threw the cans in the back and drove off.

'I tried to catch up with him, but by the time I'd reached the gate he was half-way down the track, then disappeared in a cloud of orange dust. I stood leaning on the gate for a while. Why hadn't he stopped to talk to me? What was he doing there? I couldn't believe he would steal from us.

'It was when I turned to walk back to the house that I noticed smoke curling from under the barn door - it was on fire. It hadn't rained for months and the barn was tinder dry. Within seconds I could hear the crackling and spitting of the flames as they took hold. I ran across the yard to ring the fire bell.

'The farm workers came from every direction; they grabbed the fire-buckets and formed a chain from the standpipe then across the yard to the barn. Erasmus attached a hose to the tap and trained it on the flames, while I ran back to the house to call the fire station.

'It was then I heard faint cries from the side door.'

Marisa looked at the priest, 'It was Pa, he was trapped inside. Before we could get to him the gallons of fuel stored in the barn ignited and the whole building exploded.

'The neighbours said the black smoke and flames could be seen for miles.' She looked at the priest, her eyes brimming with tears. 'The firefighters said Pa was just a petrified cinder when they found him.'

The priest, visibly shaken by her story, made the sign of the cross and murmured some words to himself, before turning to Marisa, 'My dear child this is too distressing for you, I think you should take a break now. I'm sure the officers will come soon to tell us what is holding up the proceedings. Perhaps you could call someone? Your mother?'

'No! My mother's away, and there's no-one else. She blamed me for what happened. She said that if I hadn't been so friendly with that, "black boy", he would never have been at the farm and Pa would be alive.' Marisa shook her head, 'She'd known Petrus all his life and she couldn't even say his name.' Her voice softened, 'Please, I need to tell you the rest.'

He nodded, 'Yes, I understand and whatever you say will be held in confidence.'

Marisa paced across the room, then back again, her face devoid of expression, lips pressed tightly together. When she finally spoke the priest was shocked by the bitterness in her voice.

'The police soon caught Petrus,' she spat, 'and he was taken to Bloemfontein prison. I hated him for what he had done. I wanted him to be punished and was glad he was locked up. A few weeks later I stood up in court and identified him as the one who started the fire and killed Pa. At the trial the courtroom was virtually empty. No-one was interested in just another black man accused of murder, only me and a few officials.

'I watched him in the dock. He looked terrified. Dressed in prison clothes, his face grey, shoulders sagging, he seemed to have aged ten years. I could see his eyes begging me to help him, but, how could I? He was guilty.

'The defence said Petrus knew he shouldn't have stolen the petrol, but he'd sworn on oath that he didn't know Pa was in the barn and he was also certain he didn't start the fire.

'But Petrus was no match for the lawyers; when questioned by the prosecutor he admitted he'd stubbed his cigarette out on the floor. He further agreed it was possible it was still alight and accidently ignited the straw.' She looked at the priest, and shook her head. 'He actually gave them all the information they needed to make a case against him. How dumb was that?

'Then it was my turn to take the witness stand. The prosecutor asked, "Did you see the accused go into the barn, and was he smoking?" I told him I did see Petrus go into the barn and yes, he was smoking. Then he asked me if Petrus was smoking when he came out of the barn. I told him no, he wasn't smoking.

'The next question, he said, was crucial, "Miss du Toit, did you know that your father was in the barn?" I had to say that I didn't know. However, I did say that Petrus *must* have seen him; there was nowhere to hide in that old Dutch-barn and that he'd just left Pa to die.' She looked up, 'That's what I can't forgive.

'By mid-day the trial was over. The judge found Petrus guilty of murder and sentenced him to death by hanging. As he left the dock I sensed his eyes searching for me, but I couldn't look at him. That same day he was transferred to this prison.'

Marisa turned to the priest who sat with his head bowed.

'Six months later the date of the hanging was set. So here I am. I wanted to make sure he paid for what he'd done. Ma was horrified when I told her I intended to be here, but I'm not that naïve country girl anymore. I've had three years to grow up and now I make my own decisions.'

'But you brought him flowers,' the priest said.

'Yes'

The room was quiet except for the murmuring of Father Joseph praying. Marisa sat with her eyes closed and hands clenched together, deep in thought. It was perhaps half an hour later when they heard the bell. The deep tones reverberated around the prison. Five times it tolled its solemn message, once for each condemned man.

The priest dropped to his knees, praying out loud for the souls of the dead. Marisa covered her face with her hands, her shoulders heaving with emotion.

A few minutes later the door opened and an officer entered. 'It is done,' he said. 'The public are not allowed in the execution chamber, only the executioner and the official witnesses. If you follow me I will take you to where the public announcement will be made, then if you wish you can view the coffin in the prison chapel.'

The Registrar, dressed in a black suit, stood behind a desk. He beckoned Marisa and the priest towards a row of chairs. They were the only visitors. From a black-bound book he read out four names, then the fifth - Petrus Sebezeli.

Father Joseph fingered his rosary; head bowed, eyes closed. Marisa stood up to hear the words she had waited for, yet dreaded. The Registrar adjusted his glasses and continued reading from the book. He looked directly at Marisa.

'At exactly 9.45am,' he said, 'on this day, Friday the 16th of September 1966, Petrus Sebezeli, aged twenty-four years, was gehang van die nek tot dood.' Then repeated it in English. 'At 9.45am, on this day, Friday the 16th of September 1966, Petrus Sebezeli was hanged by the neck until dead. May God rest his soul.'

He looked at Marisa, his face full of compassion, 'If you would like to view the coffin, the officer will take you.'

'Thank you.' Hands visibly shaking, Marisa picked up her bag, and with the priest at her side, followed the officer down the short corridor to the chapel.

Slowly the officer drew back a curtain to reveal a small ante-room; five simple coffins stood in a row, lids nailed down.

He pointed to the one at the far end.

'That is he,' he said. 'That is Petrus Sebelezi.'

Marisa gazed at the plain wooden box; it seemed too small to hold Petrus. She felt her lip tremble, then the tears welled up in her eyes and spilled onto her cheeks - someone had remembered her flowers and placed them on the lid.

'What happens now?' she whispered.

'There will be a short service of committal here in the prison chapel, then he'll be taken to Mamelodi cemetery and buried with the others in a pauper's grave.' He looked at Marisa, 'You don't want to go there, Miss, it's not for young ladies like you.'

'No, I won't go there. Thank you.'

'Do you want his belongings?' the officer asked, 'He only had a pair of takkies, they're still good, but there are no laces. Oh! And a photo of a young woman.' He peered at Marisa, 'she looks a bit like you,' and passed her the faded black and white photograph.

Marisa froze, 'I can't believe he kept a photo of me.'

'He must have thought a lot about you,' the priest said.

She looked at the photo - it was definitely her. Dressed in shorts and T-shirt, her dark hair in two plaits, she looked about sixteen; it bore no resemblance to the sophisticated, independent young woman she had become. She handed it back to the officer, 'Nee dankie, no thank you.'

The priest followed her down the corridor and out into the sunshine. 'What will you do now?' he asked.

'Learn to live with what I've done.'

'I don't understand.'

She turned and looked at him, her face pale and sad, 'Don't you? I wanted Petrus to pay for my father's death, but deep down I didn't really believe he'd set out to kill him.' She paused, 'And there was not really enough evidence to prove it. I also knew I could have helped him, asked for leniency. In fact, our family solicitor said that if Petrus had had a good defence lawyer the charge would certainly have been reduced to culpable homicide and he would have been awarded a custodial sentence - I could have provided that defence. 'The reality is that I am responsible for the death of my best friend. If I had taken the time to think things through then Petrus would not have hanged. And now Pa is dead, Ma has sold the farm and moved to Holland and Nomsa has gone back to her family in KwaZulu-Natal. I have no-one. She hesitated for a moment, then meeting the priest's concerned gaze added, 'But I can't turn the clock back. I will have to live with the consequences.'

The priest took her hand, 'If you ever need to talk, I am here and God will always listen. Go well my child and God bless you.'

Marisa put the car into gear and edged out of the prison gates. The city traffic was chaotic, but once on Ben Schoeman Highway she pressed the automatic convertible button. The soft-top rolled back; she felt the sun on her face, turned the radio up, and put her foot down.

The Lost Souls of Umhlanga Rocks

Do you still see the sea Marieka?
do you still see the sea?
How the white spume curled
and the sails unfurled
and we didn't have a care
as we set our course fair,
and our ship sailed gently on the tide.

Do you still see that day Marieka?
do you still see that day?
When September winds lashed
and the huge waves crashed
and we couldn't get her round
and so she ran aground,
and the rocks made a hole in her side.

Do you think of that day Marieka?
do you think of that day?
When we didn't stand a chance
in the sea's macabre dance,
how we tried a last dive
and we swam for our lives
as together we made for the shore.

Do you remember that time Marieka?
do you remember that time?
When she lay broken on the rocks
and the albatross mocked
and the waves took us down
and together we drowned,
entwined in a loving embrace.

Yes I remember that time Thembani,
yes, I remember that time.
When I lay safe in your arms
and you kept me from harm,
and I saw sorrow in your eyes
as we wept voiceless goodbyes,
our souls lost forever in time.

The Long Road to Humanity

Prologue.

The very successful rock opera, Godspell, was first produced on Broadway in 1971. In 1973 Des and Dawn Lindberg, theatre producers, staged the first racially mixed professional production in Maseru, Lesotho, to critical acclaim; it ran for five months. They then took it to South Africa to open at Wits University in Johannesburg, with a mixed cast performing to a mixed audience. It was immediately banned on the grounds of blasphemy. In reality this was widely recognised as a 'smokescreen', the real reason was one of mixing races, in direct opposition to the laws of Apartheid.

The Lindbergs sought advice from Anton Mostert, a South African lawyer, who ultimately became a judge of the Supreme Court. With his help they were able to show that the production was not in fact blasphemous, and that the Group Areas Act allowed mixed races to work together. However mixed audiences were not allowed.

With Mostert leading the case, the Lindbergs challenged the ban in the supreme court and won. This was a huge victory and set a precedent for future productions. Although mixed productions and audiences were still against the law, it became an accepted practice and was the start of a new approach to multi-racial performances and audience.

Johannesburg 1974

I have never shied away from a challenge, so when Thandie invited me to the controversial multi-racial production of the rock opera, Godspell, I accepted.

I first met Thandie at an anti-apartheid rally; a white South African and retired teacher, she's quiet and calm with a strong faith in God. At the age of sixty-three she's more than thirty years older than me and yet we share a sense of humour and an interest in politics and the theatre.

Fearless in her support for human rights she's well known to the Bureau of State Security for her involvement with the Black Sash Movement; she made it clear there may be repercussions.

'There is likely to be heightened security,' she warned, 'which may make things difficult for you, Jennie. I'm often followed by the security police and I'm quite sure my phone is tapped. The government don't want this production to go ahead. They'll be checking passes and ID cards of everyone in the audience and will arrest anyone they suspect is a subversive. Once your name is on their books you will be watched, so I understand if you would rather not take the risk.'

I knew the South African government had originally banned the production on the grounds of blasphemy and that the ban was overturned by the supreme court. I also knew the tickets were like gold dust. 'It will be held in a converted barn on a farm about thirty miles north of Johannesburg,' Thandie explained, 'admission is strictly by invitation only.'

I suppose I did feel a little anxious, but I couldn't let her down, in any case I was really looking forward to seeing this controversial performance. It caused such a stir when it opened that the whole of Johannesburg was talking about it. So, crouching over the steering wheel, legs stretched fully to reach the pedals, I put the Land Rover into reverse and back Big Bertha onto the road.

I don't like the long lonely unlit road; no cat's eyes, no road markings, just two narrow beams of light keeping me to the linear strips of tarmac. The blackness envelopes me and when headlights flash behind me I'm half glad there's life out there and half afraid it means danger.

It's at least an hour's drive to the farm, through a lonely expanse of veld, and already my stomach's churning. My sweaty palms, damp with trepidation, slip on the steering wheel; I force myself to take a few deep breaths. A hazy string of lights on the horizon bring relief, but as the temporary theatre comes into view I see a significant police presence, a threatening force inciting fear.

In my anxiety I almost run over the gun-toting policeman who's jumped in front of Big Bertha. I wind the window down, 'Sorry Officer.'

'Park your vehicle over there,' he barks in a heavy Afrikaans accent and points to an adjacent field, 'and watch where you're going.'

As I walk towards the converted barn the air is cool on my face and I inhale the sweet perfume of jasmine and frangipane. I can hear the rat-a-tat-a-tat of drums beating out a welcome and a gospel choir starts to sing.

Outside the makeshift theatre the excited crowd dance and sway to the music, black and white together in friendship, and the big fat bottoms of the mammas wobble and giggle to the rhythm.

The atmosphere is all I hoped it would be. 'It's going to be okay,' I tell myself as I join in the dancing, much to the amusement of the young girls in Xhosa dress selling programmes.

I can't see Thandie, so I join the long queue already snaking round the building; my heart sinks as it divides into two lines. I'm guided by marshals towards the queue on the right, but as I near the door I see the familiar sign:

Ingang net Blankes...Entrance Whites only.

The black people follow the sign to the left,

Ingang net Swartes...Entrance Blacks only,

Inside the auditorium I take my seat with the Whites. It is a multi-racial audience, but a segregated one; Whites on one side, Blacks on the other. Apartheid lives on.

The curtains open to a minimalistic stage setting. Devoid of colour everything is black, white, or grey; a couple of benches and a table complete the set. A chicken wire fence  displaying the warning sign, DANGER...ELECTRIFIED, outlines the perimeter of the stage. My stomach churns with excitement and just a hint of fear.

The first half, a joyful cacophony of song, dance, stories, and parables, reflects the colourful vibrancy of the African culture and promotes a message of goodness, love and forgiveness. It receives rapturous applause. But as the lights go up I'm shocked to see armed police officers, with Alsatian dogs, patrolling behind the fence. An actor, dressed in long white robes, walks on to the stage. He's followed by the rest of the cast carrying trestle tables laden with glasses and baskets of bread.

He addresses the audience.

'My friends,' holding his arms out as if to embrace each and every one of us.

'To celebrate this multi-racial performance of Godspell, I invite you all to join me and the cast on the stage. Come, take wine and break bread with me.'

The theatre is buzzing with anticipation. As requested the audience forms two separate, orderly queues - Blacks and Whites. I join the white queue. To my horror my fears are realised, the black people are turned away by the police. But in an astonishing show of solidarity, everyone, black and white, are returning to their seats in dignified silence.

I can see Thandie now; tall and statuesque, her shock of unruly white hair is unmistakeable. She's standing at the front, bridging the space between the segregated races.

Softly she starts to sing that well-known psalm, 'The Lord is my Shepherd'. The swaying audience joins in. The haunting music rises to a smooth rich crescendo, filling the theatre with sorrow and hope. My body's tingling. Anticipation is replaced with apprehension and my deep-rooted religious scepticism is shaken by the seismic power of this demonstration of faith. I'm overawed by Thandie's courage.

The final act is about to be portrayed. The stage is dimly lit. I sense an air of defiance, a new energy and determination. Spotlights snap and focus on Jesus. He's a slip of a boy, white and naked except for a loin cloth and a crown of thorns. He hangs, head bowed, crucified on the wire fence.

The lights switch and train on six powerful Zulus. They remove the body with gentle reverence, then hold Jesus aloft on outstretched hands, his face upturned, as if offering him to God. His limbs hang loose. The scene is shocking in its simplicity; the impact electrifying.

Slowly the tableau moves towards the steps and down into a stunned audience. This wasn't in the script. There are gasps. I gasp. People are trying to touch the actors as if to draw strength and courage. The tension is palpable. The police shuffle nervously; I sense they're ready to step in, but they back off. And so I stand shoulder to shoulder with the people, just ordinary people who are not afraid. I hear their cheers, see their tears and I weep with them.

The performance ends and the police channel the audience into lines. I'm ushered out with the Whites; their sober faces reflect the sombre mood. The Blacks remain seated, waiting for permission to leave. Thandie is standing with them, calm and dignified. I acknowledge her with a nod and a sad smile, ashamed I'm not brave enough to join her.

Imperceptibly she shakes her head, warning me not to acknowledge her. I see two officers walking towards her; there's nothing I can do, so I turn and walk away into the dark night.

Almost immediately I'm stopped by a flashlight, 'Identity card,' the officer demands. Silently I hand it over. He scrutinises it with his torch, 'Name?'

'Jennie Powell.'

'Race?'

'White European.'

'Report to the police station tomorrow,' he orders, thrusting a docket in my hand.

As I drive into the blackness the headlights pick out a makeshift poster pasted on the door.

THIS PRODUCTION IS CANCELLED
UNTIL FURTHER NOTICE.

I press my foot down hard on the accelerator; Big Bertha responds without hesitation. The black night seems less frightening, the road's still lonely and dark and there are no cat's eyes to show the way - it's just a long straight road that leads to home and hope.

As I open the door I can hear the phone ringing. I recognise the quiet voice of Andre, Thandie's husband.

'Jennie?'

'Yes Andre.'

'She is safely home.'

That's all I need to know, for now. Tomorrow's papers will report a success; I will know the truth.

The Way to Peace

When terror reigns and all the world looks on,
and all the world can see those evil deeds.
When all pretence of civil rights is gone
and no-one cares to help the ones in need.

When children cry and no-one dries their tears,
and violence takes the form of faceless men.
When no-one hears the voice of those in fear
then trust is gone and hope is lost again.

Then will the world unite and fight for peace,
and evil will be vanquished from our lands,
and truth and light will rise and wars will cease,
and bombs and guns will be for ever banned.

And in the final days the world will find
that peaceful words, not wars, did save mankind.

Glossary

Ag shame	You poor thing.
Apartheid	System of racial segregation and discrimination in South Africa between 1948 and 1991
Bakkie	Small truck
Blanke	White
Dagga	Cannabis
Dongas	Ditch
Gogga	Generic for biting insects. eg. Mosquito
Kleintjie	Little one
Koeksisters	Deep-fried dough, twisted into plaits
Lekker	Good/nice
Ligte uit	Lights out
Molo	Hello
Muti	Medicine
Ouma	Grandma
Protea	South Africa's National Flower.
Rondavel	Round-shaped hut, usually thatched
Sjambok	Truncheon
Stoep	Veranda
Strelitzia	Flower, also known as Bird of Paradise
Swarts	Black
Takkies	Canvas shoes/trainers
Tokoloshe	Mischievous imp, sprite
Tsotsis	Street gangs
Totsiens	Goodbye
Sangoma	Witchdoctor
Unjani?	How are you?
Uncedo	Help
Voetsek	Impolite way of saying 'get lost'